A Portal in Time

Claire Fullerton

Claire Fullerton

Vinspire Publishing
Ladson, South Carolina
www.vinspirepublishing.com

A Portal in Time

ISBN: 978-0-9890632-2-7

PUBLISHED BY VINSPIRE PUBLISHING, LLC

To my husband, William Barton Feil who told me to use my imagination.

Prologue

September 23, 1907
Carmel, California

She walked down the lane, braced against the gusting wind twisting her skirt into tangles around her ankles. Sweeping her hair to the left, she clasped it firmly in the same hand that held the top of her cloak. Determinedly, she marched forward until the lane veered to a sharp right and headed straight down to the sea. When she reached the place where the lane met the sand, she leaned over quickly and removed her lace-up shoes. Securing them tightly in her right hand, she walked onto the beach, barely breaking its surface.

The waves came forward in a mounting swell and with their forward progression, more of the beach disappeared into the steel-gray of the Pacific Ocean. It was the end of the day, and the tide labored forcibly beneath the fading blue sky. She stood listening intently to the fury of the wind as it intermittently drowned out the pulsating rhythm of the sea. Gathering herself, she turned to the right, to the place in the water she had come to see.

Shielding her eyes from the setting sun, Valeria Sienna Kristiansen steadied her gaze and spoke into the wind as a chill began to creep up her spine.

"This place will now be a portal in time."

Chapter One

September 21, 2000
Carmel, California

It was three o'clock on a crisp fall day when Anna and Kevin Townsend checked into the Madeira Hotel in Carmel, California. They stood side by side at the reception desk as the smiling young man behind it handed over two keys.

"And if you would like anything, anything at all, just dial zero, and we'll be happy to accommodate you," he said with an air of professional courtesy.

"Thank you, we will." Anna smiled back as she scanned the brochures grouped together in stainless steel stands along the right side of the desk. Her gaze touched on and was immediately drawn to a brochure with a black-and-white sketch of the hotel on the outside and an account of its history on the inside.

"It feels kind of old here, doesn't it?" Anna studied the drawing. "It says here this hotel was built in stages, beginning at the turn of the nineteenth century."

"Probably one of the first hotels built in the area, if that's the case. Most of Carmel was settled afterwards." Kevin took charge of their suitcases and started walking towards the back of the lobby.

Anna pivoted slowly, allowing her interest to sweep the breadth of the foyer that flowed into the opulent lobby. She walked into the lobby and stood still, letting the feel of the space permeate her skin. Anna liked to try on new environments the way most women like to try on new clothes. Whenever she was in a new place, she liked to pretend she lived there. She allowed her imagination to run free and would try on her surroundings the way an actor slips into character by putting on a costume. She marveled at how easy it was to pretend in the entrance of this hotel.

Everything in the lobby was exquisite. A coral-colored rug covered most of the sandstone floor, and delicate porcelain pieces graced mahogany tables sitting beside upholstered arrangements in front of a marble fireplace. As she stood in front of the fireplace, her glance traveled to the front where an enticing Mediterranean-tiled staircase swept up in a subtle curve to the level above. A stained-glass window, cut in the shape of a star, resided halfway up the stairs, and she imagined herself looking through it as she walked with her hand on the wrought-iron rail.

She shook herself out of her reverie and followed Kevin down a short flight of stairs that led to a glass-paned door in the back of the lobby. Through the door, spacious formal gardens rested on a hill facing the ocean. Fuchsia bougainvillea lined the walls of the garden and vibrant colors erupted in floral patterns everywhere. A manicured lawn traveled throughout the strategically placed flowerbeds, and a walkway of worn russet bricks trailed through the maze and led them straight to the door of their room.

Anna rushed into the room after Kevin opened the door. "Look at this," she exclaimed. "This is great!"

Kevin pulled Anna into a hug. "I'm glad you like it."

"I love it. It's like being in an enchanted cottage by

the sea. Look at this room. It's fabulous! We can even hear the ocean from inside!"

"Happy anniversary weekend," Kevin said, and the look on his face told Anna he was buoyed by her happiness.

"You know, technically, after tomorrow we won't be newlyweds anymore," Anna countered.

"That's right, after tomorrow it's all over," Kevin agreed.

"It's been great growing old with you so far."

"You too." Kevin flashed his quick smile. "Since time is marching on so quickly, we better put our stuff down and get going. What do you want to do first?"

"I guess look around the hotel for a bit and then head into the village before the sun sets. It's great to be back in Carmel, isn't it?"

"Back to the scene of the crime," Kevin joked.

"Our wedding was a crime? Excuse me?" Anna knew exactly what Kevin meant because she was so familiar with his sense of humor, but still she feigned indignation just for the sport of it.

"It's only an expression, and anyway I'm kidding."

"Many thanks, I appreciate that. Just so you know, from now on my plan is to return to the scene of the crime every year on our anniversary," Anna informed him.

"That's the plan?"

"That's the plan. You know I'm big on tradition. You have to use it whenever you can find it, and it's never too late to start."

"Or create a new tradition," Kevin added.

"Exactly," Anna agreed.

"Good idea. That's one of the things I like about you the best."

"Good. We can talk about the thousands of other things you like about me later. Time's wasting." She searched around for the best place to park her suitcase.

The room was spacious, bright, and uncluttered in its furnishings. It contained a king-size bed draped in white linen, two wooden bedside tables, a freestanding armoire painted with a peach-colored trim that matched the color of the walls perfectly, and a small seating arrangement that sat before the front window. Fashioned completely out of large white-marble tiles, the bathroom had a European feel to it due to the long, narrow, high-sided bathtub.

Anna was pleased with the arrangement and turning again to Kevin she asked, "Aren't you glad we came?"

"Of course I am. Are you ready to get going?"

"Let's go." Anna pocketed the room key and opened the door.

They walked outside and headed back into the lobby, and this time Anna took her time looking at every detail within the room. She peered closely at the collection of maps grouped on the wall and recognized many that depicted Carmel at the turn of the nineteenth century, while some represented the present day.

Some of the black-and-white photographs portrayed the various stages the hotel had gone through in its growth. Others showed the town of Carmel in its early stages, with unpaved roads and hitching posts where horses stood tied. Women posed in long dresses, wearing lace-up boots, and holding parasols to shield them from the sun. Men wore hats, and coats with matching vests, and some sported walking canes. The photographs hung throughout the lobby and flowed into the back of the hotel where there were three more large rooms with more photographs depicting the same era.

Anna moved silently through the rooms, studying the frames closely. "As many times as we've been to Carmel, it's funny it took us so long to notice this hotel." Anna walked over to Kevin, who stood loading film into his camera.

"This hotel's a little off the beaten path. It's not that easy to find because this is the residential area of Carmel. I think that's what took us so long to come across it. We've always stayed in the center of things so we could walk everywhere."

"That's probably it," Anna said and nodded. "I'm not complaining about southern California, but I like it so much better up here. I just like everything about the environment better. It's got a feel to it here that I can't find in L.A. Heavier, denser, more historic, and a little moodier."

"The grass is always greener, right?"

"Yeah, kind of." Anna took Kevin by the arm and led him over to one of the photographs that hung on the wall. "Look at these people here. Don't they all look kind of eerie?"

"That's just the way they developed photographs back then," Kevin explained.

"Maybe that's part of it, but I keep thinking all of the people in these photographs are no longer living. It's like looking at a gallery of ghosts."

"That's an unusual thought. They're probably connected with the hotel in some way."

"No doubt. We should ask someone who works here to tell us their story."

Chapter Two

June 1, 1902
San Francisco, California

Valeria Sienna was overjoyed when her father ultimately consented to the idea of Anders Kristiansen calling upon her. Nervously, she had waited for a window of opportunity to ask for his permission, and she had found it in the hour just after his return from work.

It was a mild early-summer evening, and her father sat alone in the drawing room in his leather winged-back chair, with a tumbler of Scotch whisky at his right and a freshly lit cigar balanced between his thumb and forefinger. It was how he observed the end of most workdays, and he appeared to be lost in his thoughts.

"Father?" Valeria stood at the drawing room door. "May I disturb you for a moment?" She entered the large, lavishly decorated room and closed the heavy mahogany double doors behind her. She turned again and walked softly, stopping a reverent distance before meeting his gaze.

Domenico Sienna, as he was known in the business world, put his cigar in the crystal ashtray that gleamed upon the cherry-wood side table and stood up slowly, as was his habit when a female entered the room. Tightening his favorite burgundy smoking jacket—the one sent to him by her uncle in northern Italy who owned his own cigar shop—he held out his hand to Valeria. "Of course. Please sit with me."

Valeria perched lightly upon the serpentine-backed Sheraton sofa and crossed her legs at her ankles. She folded her hands in her lap for a moment but then immediately began to smooth the creases in her long white linen skirt.

"I've had a calling card just this day sent to me from a young man Mother and I met at the art gallery two days ago. I'd like to tell you about him."

"The art gallery? You and your mother fraternized with a stranger at the art gallery?"

"Yes," Valeria confirmed.

"And who is he, this young man with the calling card? An admirer of art? A curator perhaps, or is he simply a stranger in the crowd admiring your beauty?"

Valeria's cheeks burned. "Mrs. Davenworth from Pacific Heights introduced him to Mother and me quite properly."

"Mrs. Davenworth?" He nodded, looking at her with a steady gaze under raised eyebrows. "What more do you have to tell of him?"

"He is a painter himself, not long in San Francisco. His name is Mr. Anders Kristiansen."

"And he sent his calling card?"

"Yes."

"And do you know where he is from? Who are his people? What about his connections, does he have any?"

"As I said, he is not from here." She wished they could move quickly through this part of the conversation.

"Where then?" her father inquired.

"Norway." Valeria fidgeted in her seat trying to sit up taller. "Where Mrs. Davenworth grew up. He knows her uncle, and I believe Mrs. Davenworth is his champion."

"Norway," her father repeated in a voice that implied there would be no further reason to pursue the subject. He picked up his cigar and walked across the drawing room to the cathedral doors that led out into the side garden. "I'll open these now."

The air blew into the room, shaping the white muslin window treatment into billows that floated just inches above the dark wooden floor. Throughout the room, rich area rugs of crimson, green, and gold covered the floor.

Valeria waited, knowing the next word was his.

"Norway," he said again. "Not Italy, not even America."

"No, Father," she confessed, looking down at the floor below her feet.

"And he wants to call upon you," he stated as he walked to his chair and sat down again.

"Yes, he does, and I would be happy to receive him…with your permission."

Her father continued to stare at Valerie intently. He did not present an imposing figure, yet there was an undeniable formidable quality about him. Five feet ten inches tall, with pitch-black hair that belied his fifty-eight years, he had black eyes that seemed all the more intense due to the fact that they were set back beneath tight eyelids and lay under heavy black brows. With a finely chiseled face, her sire had the look of a stern man, yet he was not. He was thoughtful, serious, methodical, and dependable, and within his great capacity to love, there lay the ever-present awareness of action and its attendant consequences.

A native of Naples, Italy, her father had immigrated

to San Francisco in 1870, seeking to make his fortune. He had done just that through painstaking hard work, by setting up a coffee shop which evolved into a grocery store, and after a handful of successful years, he bought a twenty room hotel named the Genoa and incrementally improved its value. By the time Valeria was born in 1884, her father was considered one of San Francisco's richest men, and the family enjoyed great prosperity while living in a large Victorian house on Nob Hill.

Though he fully embraced the American way of life, he remained ever mindful of his homeland, which caused him to send his two sons to Italy for their education and inspired him to serve as a representative of Italy at official events in San Francisco. Although his acquaintances and business associates were of varied ethnicities, the people he kept closest to him were all Italian, for he maintained a healthy suspicion of outsiders and a fierce loyalty to those he considered to be members of his extended family.

"Father, with your permission, I could write to Mr. Kristiansen and ask him to call on me this Saturday for four o'clock tea. You could meet him then," Valeria proposed.

"It is unusual your suitor did not seek my permission first, but since he has met your mother I must assume words of encouragement were exchanged?"

"Oh, yes. I have already spoken to Mother, and she counseled me to bring the matter directly to you."

Her father picked up his drink, and although he did not seem completely enamored of the proposition, he turned to Valeria. "It sounds to me as if we have your mother's approval, and we both know that I begrudge you little. I see no harm in this, so, yes, Mr. Kristiansen may call upon you."

Valeria leaped to her feet, threw her arms around her father, thanked him profusely, and shot out of the room at lightning speed before he could change his mind. She hurried to the middle of the black-and-white marble entrance hall and looked up to the top of the double winding stairs.

"Francesca, where are you?" Valeria shouted, she hoped her sister was in the upstairs sitting room. When she did not hear an answering shout back, she wheeled around to the front door, opened it wide, and scanned the vastness of the front yard.

Convinced Francesca was not out front, she raced across the full length of the entrance hall, through the rectangular dining room, and into the spacious stone kitchen.

"Maria, have you seen Francesca?" she called to the family's cook while reaching for the glass-paned door leading out to the western garden.

"She's out there," Maria returned.

In half a second, she was through the door, calling out into the garden. "Francesca!"

"What is it?" a voice from below called back.

Valeria skipped down the red brick stairs leading to the greenhouse and found her sister inside. Francesca stood wearing white canvas gloves that reached well past her wrists as she inspected a row of potted orchids. Valeria closed the door behind her.

"Which one is that?" Valeria blurted out, surprised at herself for not blurting out her own news.

"*Epidendrum alatum*, but you can call it winged

epidendrum. Look at the rich yellow color." Francesca poured water from a patinaed copper can and looked at her sister.

"You'll never guess what Father said," Valeria enthused.

"He no doubt gave you exactly what you asked for, which means Father said yes," Francesca returned without hesitation.

"He did, and I am so pleased. Will you help me draft a note to Mr. Kristiansen? You're so much better at these things than I am. He's invited to tea this Saturday. You'll be here, won't you?"

"Of course I'll be here if you want me to be. What did Mother say?"

"I haven't told her yet, but she knew I was going to ask for Father's permission. Mr. Kristiansen charmed Mother as well as me, so I know she'll be happy Father said yes."

"Mother may be the one surprised to hear of Father's agreement," Francesca remarked as she continued moving from one orchid to the next. "Did Father ask you if your suitor was Italian?"

"He did not have to because I told him his name before he had the chance to ask."

Francesca laughed. "Clever of you."

"No, not at all. I was too nervous to be clever," Valeria confided.

"I imagine you were. The worst is behind you now. We'll go together and tell Mother, and then I will help you draft the note." Francesca smiled.

Her sister was only three years older than Valeria, but her innate wisdom went well beyond her twenty-one years. Beauty, dignity, graciousness, and maturity were all attributes Francesca could claim, and Valeria adored her. Francesca was Valeria's guide and confidant, and their relationship lacked any trace of sisterly competitiveness.

Instead, she considered her sister to be a maternal figure, for although their mother was warm-hearted in nature, she possessed a subtly aloof temperament. While Valeria revered her genteel and beautiful mother who adhered to many of the customs and traditions of her native Italy, she knew, in her eyes, children were to emulate the leadership of their parents without question. However, Valeria was not a blind follower by nature. She related to her mother with the utmost respect but brought all of her questions, comments, and opinions to Francesca, who humored her with unending patience.

The heartfelt bond connecting them to each other fostered emotional support and unconditional love. With their similarities in looks, both possessing the dark hair and eyes of their father and the long slender frame of their mother, at a glance she and Francesca looked as if they could have been identical twins, but there the similarities ended.

Valeria was athletic, outgoing, impulsive, and inquisitive, while Francesca was constant, steady, reserved, and demure. Valeria enthusiastically embraced horseback riding, archery, and ballet, whereas Francesca preferred reading, needlepoint, knitting, and gardening. Combined, they possessed the gamut of a well-rounded life, and they reveled in their differences and saw themselves as halves of a whole. They traded clothes, hair clasps, parasols, and jewelry, and neither gave a thought to personally possessing any article the other could not share.

Arm in arm, they went to find their mother, who stood reading from a handwritten list in the kitchen. The evening's meal being already underway, her list contained instructions for the next day's menu. Their mother believed in being a day ahead when it came to all of her concerns.

Adriana smiled distractedly at her daughters and interrupted her instructions long enough to say, "Dinner will be served in half an hour, girls. I expect I'll see you both washed and dressed momentarily?"

"Yes, Mother," they said in unison.

"Valeria has spoken to Father," Francesca began.

"I've just come from your father's side, and he spoke of your conversation." Their mother handed her list to their cook. "I understand Mr. Kristiansen will be joining us for tea?"

"Yes, Mother, this Saturday." Valeria brimmed with excitement.

"I see the subject has brought color to your face. It suits you, my love." She reached out and placed a tender hand on Valeria's cheek. "I think we should speak little else of Mr. Kristiansen to your father until the day arrives. He is a busy man with a thousand things on his mind."

"Of course not, Mother. Francesca will help me write to Mr. Kristiansen. I'll be so grateful if you could review the note before we have it delivered."

"It will be my pleasure. Now run along girls, let's not keep your father waiting for his dinner."

Valeria bolted up the entrance hall stairs ahead of

her sister and ran straight into the upstairs sitting room at the top of the landing.

"Francesca," Valeria's voice wafted back, "I'm in here, please join me, and we shall write to Mr. Kristiansen."

Francesca crossed the threshold of the sitting room that adjoined Valeria's room to hers. She walked over to the ottoman positioned before the fireplace and sat down, rustling through the andirons beside the fire and stoking its flames. "There is no urgency. We have plenty of time to do this, and we will have to think carefully."

"Francesca, you are going to dampen my enthusiasm." Valeria sat poised before the writing desk with a pen in her hand.

Francesca laughed. "We both know it is impossible to dampen your enthusiasm. Be that as it may, let me see what you have in mind."

Valeria quickly drafted the invitation and handed it to Francesca. The note read:

Mr. Kristiansen,

Please accept our invitation to join us for four o'clock tea this forthcoming Saturday.

We look forward to your presence and send kind regards.

The Domenico Sienna family

Chapter Three

September 21, 2000
Carmel

Anna walked back through the lobby and approached the hotel's front desk. The young man who had registered them earlier was still in attendance. He took his hands off the computer keyboard and stepped to the right of his monitor.

"Hello again," Anna began, smiling. "My husband and I were just looking at all of the photographs in the lobby, and I was wondering if anybody here could answer a few questions about them."

"Certainly, Mrs. Townsend." He picked up the phone and a moment later a door opened from behind the desk. A tall, dignified man wearing a tweed coat and tortoiseshell glasses walked to the desk. The clerk introduced them. "Mrs. Townsend, this is Nigel Matthews, our hotel manager."

"How can I assist you?" The manager stood erect with a steady gaze and a regal English accent.

"I was wondering if anybody could give me a bit of background on some of the photographs hanging on the wall." She pointed towards the back of the hotel.

"I would be more than happy to help. If you would allow me a moment?"

"Yes, of course. My husband is just over there so when you are ready, come and join us."

Within five minutes, Nigel walked towards Anna

and Kevin, carrying what looked to be two large cream-colored photograph albums.

"This is the man I told you about," Anna whispered quickly to Kevin.

Kevin extended his right hand, saying, "I'm Kevin Townsend." The two men shook hands.

"Nigel Matthews, at your service."

"My wife is interested in these vintage photographs."

"Yes, eventually most of our guests grow curious over the photos, so I've come prepared. Are you a photographer then, or is it the subject matter that intrigues you?" Nigel turned towards Anna.

"The subject matter."

"Ah, well then, perhaps it's best we start over here." Nigel led the way deeper into the back hallway and stood before a sepia-tinted photograph of a two-story sandstone house. It stood on an unpaved road nestled among a group of immature pine trees. The house looked unspectacular by most accounts, being moderate in size and possessing only one window in the front, but its location was desirable, with a view that rambled unobstructed to the sea.

"This photograph was taken in 1905 at the completion of the house's construction. We stand here before a picture taken of the first stage of this hotel."

Anna shot Kevin a quick, surprised glance and threw her attention back to Nigel, who sounded to be at the beginning of a prepared oration.

"If you will just glance here," Nigel pointed to his left, "you'll see the architectural plans of the house drafted by the original owner. He was a painter by the name of Kristiansen who enjoyed a grand reputation in these parts for his watercolors. He became, in fact, the most popular artist in the region during the height of his career. This house was his residence and you may have noticed it is not fashioned in the typical way as others in this area. His wife, you see, was of Italian lineage, so Kristiansen's aspiration was to emulate the style of houses found in the Italian countryside then add a bit of Spanish influence to the mix."

"What part of the hotel is made up of the original house?" Anna queried.

"Why, the part we're standing in now. This was the hallway before the kitchen, so the three of us would actually be in the back of the house. The lobby, of course, and the stairs to the right of the front door are part of the original house, as is the star-shaped stained-glass window you see as you ascend the staircase."

"That window is gorgeous," Anna said.

"Yes, the star shape is found repeatedly throughout Carmel. It's reminiscent of the window over the door of the main chapel of the Spanish mission, which was built in 1770 at the edge of Carmel Valley. Have you been down there yet?"

"Yes, we've walked all around the mission," Kevin inserted. "We've been to Carmel about four times before. In fact, we were married here just last year."

"So you've seen the window's prototype. It is an icon in Carmel. One can easily see why Kristiansen would want to copy it for his own home," Nigel stated.

"A thing of beauty is an endless fascination no matter where you place it, that's what I've always said," Kevin added.

"It's a creative touch," Anna agreed.

"Yes, well, Kristiansen was the creative sort and so was his wife. They were both painters, and today we recognize them as being significant patrons of the arts during the early days of Carmel's existence. I've taken the liberty of bringing along these albums for your perusal. We've assembled quite a collection of photographs and periodicals that illustrate the reincarnation this house has experienced in order to become today's Madeira Hotel. The photographs hanging throughout the lobby depict the early days of Carmel's history, and as you review the contents of these albums, you'll come to understand the environment during the hotel's inception." Nigel extended the albums to Anna, who gratefully accepted them.

"Should I return these to the front desk when we're finished?"

"That would be splendid." Nigel turned to go. "I'll leave you to it, then."

"Thank you, nice to meet you, we appreciate it," Anna and Kevin said in overlapping unison.

"Shall we *peruse*, then?" Anna said in her best English accent.

"You're not making fun of the guy, are you? He's a nice guy."

"I'm only kidding. Come on. Do you want to flip through these albums?"

"I don't know, Anna, it's getting kind of late and if you want to walk into the village before dinner, maybe we should give these to the guy at the front desk and then come back for them later."

"Good point," Anna agreed. "What time is it?"

"Just a little after five."

"Okay, let me give these back to the concierge."

Outside, a few minutes later, she turned and walked over to the star-shaped stained-glass window, angling her way behind the thick bushes that grew flush against the front of the hotel to stand beneath it. She reached up, but couldn't quite touch the glass.

"Anna, what are you doing?"

"I'm fascinated by this window. Look at the colors. There's green, blue, red, and if you narrow your eyes a little, there's a bit of gold. How old did Nigel say this window was?"

"It's part of the original building so probably about a hundred years old. Why do you have to put your hands on it?"

"I just want to feel it, that's all," she explained.

Chapter Four

June 6, 1998
Los Angeles

Kevin, after knowing Anna for the past two and a half years, was at the point where he knew when to leave well enough alone. She was going to do what she was going to do and any input from him would only lead to a circular conversation with the end result being the same. It was as if the two had diametrically opposed ways of dealing with the world. Kevin, being extremely cautious, approached all things with studious forethought. Anna only knew how to plunge right into the middle of things. She was impulsive, creative, inquisitive, and unpredictable, and these characteristics contributed to her overall appeal.

With her long, straight, jet-black hair and piercing green eyes, Anna was the polar opposite of Kevin in all things that seemingly mattered when one considered the laws of attraction. Rather than being challenged, she'd completely intrigued him.

Anna mesmerized Kevin from the start, when he had first set eyes on her in the elevator of the Mid-Wilshire apartment building where they both lived in Los Angeles. It was at the end of the day, the first week of June. They had entered the elevator simultaneously and reached for the same button to the sixth floor.

Kevin had taken a step back, apologizing for nearly stepping on her toes. It was then he had taken a closer look at what she carried in her arms. A large pitch-black short-haired cat with yellow-green eyes peeked out from beneath Anna's waist-length hair, and Kevin stared as he tried to decipher which coat of hair belonged to whom. Anna stood looking straight ahead as if it were the most natural thing in the world to be carrying a cat in an elevator.

When they arrived at the sixth floor, the doors parted and they both stepped out but headed in opposite directions. He turned to his left as he opened his apartment door, wanting to get another glimpse of Anna and curious about which apartment was hers. Hers was the one in the corner and with no hesitation he closed his apartment door and hurried after her.

"Excuse me," Kevin said.

Anna turned with a ready smile. She didn't seem surprised in the least.

"I've recently moved here. I noticed you have a lot of sunflowers out on your balcony. The person who lived here before me left a huge plant on my balcony, and I've almost succeeded in killing it. I don't know what to do other than water it every so often. I feel guilty that it's in such pitiful shape. I thought I'd ask you for a little advice."

"What kind of a plant?" Anna put her cat down and gently coaxed it inside. "Go on in, Franny, I'll be there in a minute." The cat looked up at Anna as if it spoke her language.

"Well, I'm not really sure," Kevin confessed.

"What kind of water are you using?" Anna continued.

"What kind of water? I didn't know there were

different kinds. What should I be using?" Kevin wondered aloud.

"I wouldn't use tap water, not here in L.A. In fact, if I were you, I wouldn't use the tap water for anything beyond washing."

"Okay, maybe that's it."

Anna narrowed her eyes. "Do you like the plant?"

"Yes. Well, no, not really," Kevin answered, thinking it was a funny question. "What I mean is, I'm not very good with plants, but I feel some kind of a moral obligation not to kill this one since it's already out there."

"Well, you inherited the plant. What matters most is if you like it, because it's going to know."

"Who is going to know?"

"The plant. It knows. It can feel if you're happy to have it or not."

Kevin began to follow her point. "Oh, you mean I should be one of those guys who talks to plants?"

"It's actually a little more than just talking. It's the attitude you have when you're around it. Plants are alive, you know. Anything that's alive can feel," she stated.

"Right, okay, water and attitude."

Anna was cute, and wasn't anything like the girls back home in Massachusetts, but Kevin had already heard a little something about Californians and their new-age mentality.

"Good, give it a try." She smiled at him as if that concluded things.

"I will, thanks. Sorry to bother you." Kevin backed away.

"Not at all." She entered her apartment and gently closed the door.

Kevin walked down the hall. After unlocking the door, he threw his keys on the kitchen table and walked out onto the balcony—glancing briefly in the direction of Anna's apartment.

She looks to be about twenty. She's probably from here, based on her accent. What a strange color of eyes she has, beautiful-strange. They match her cat's eyes. She looks like her cat – something feline about her, that's for sure.

His mind filled with thoughts of Anna, and for the next two weeks Kevin hoped to run into her every time he left or returned to his apartment.

* * *

On the third week of June, Kevin shut down his computer and closed his office door at the Century City law firm of Williams and Khan. He brushed his hair from his forehead and reached in his suit pocket, looking for the note with the address of a restaurant in Beverly Hills called Max's. He knew how to get there, or at least he thought he did. It wasn't that far away from his apartment. Jim Thorpe, another lawyer at the firm, had suggested they meet there for a drink after work.

He pulled over on Canon Drive and began looking for a parking space. *It must be somewhere in this block,* he thought as his vision swept left and right looking for a vacant parking meter. He circled the block three times before he gave up and pulled over before the front door of Max's. He closed the door to his dark green Jeep and handed his keys to the valet, cautioning the man to tread lightly in second gear.

He didn't like valet parking, something he rarely had to succumb to back home in Chatham, Massachusetts, and he maintained a sneaking suspicion he would find his car somehow altered upon his return. Brushing the thought off for lack of an alternative, he stepped to the side as a short man wearing a top hat held open the door to Max's.

Jim Thorpe waited for Kevin at the bar. Several white linen tables set with crystal and stainless steel sat in the adjoining room, and a brass winding staircase swirled up to the second floor at the far end of the restaurant.

Jim stood up to greet Kevin. "Have you ever been here before?"

"No, never, but that's not saying a lot. I've only been in Los Angeles for about seven weeks." Kevin pulled up a tall bar stool and sat beside Jim.

"I couldn't afford to come to Beverly Hills when I was in law school, much less a place like this, but now that I'm gainfully employed, I figured I'd milk it." Jim winked one of his twinkling blue eyes.

"Well then, I'll do as the locals do. When in Rome and all that," Kevin said.

"Okay, what's your poison?"

"Do they have imported beer?"

"They have just about anything you can imagine." Jim pointed to the display of bottles behind the bar.

The bartender threw a cocktail napkin onto the bar in front of Kevin. "What will you have?"

"I'll have a Hansa, if you have it."

"What's that, Norwegian?" Jim asked enthusiastically. "Awfully highbrow of you."

"Not really, more like awfully expensive. You wouldn't believe the taxes the government puts on beer in Norway. I've spent quite a lot of time there. My

Mother's from Norway."

"Do tell," Jim said with interest.

"Yeah, she's been in America for close to thirty years though. Her family's still there. She's great. She's a painter. Anyway, I've spent just about every summer of my life in Norway."

Jim shook his head, laughing. "You were raised by a Norwegian artist? I just don't see it. Of course, there is that long hair of yours. I could be wrong." Jim laughed again.

"Hey, just because I'm a lawyer doesn't mean I can't have long hair or be the son of an artist." Kevin laughed along with him.

"You've got a point, counselor, and I bet the women love every strand on your blond head. I've noticed Janine seems to be all over you."

"The receptionist? No thanks." Kevin took a long swallow of his beer and thought of the woman with the big hair who wore way too much makeup. "Not my type."

"How's your plant?" A voice floated over Kevin's shoulder. He turned and set his beer mug on the bar, meeting Anna's gaze.

"It's you!" The words flew from his mouth. "Jim, this is…I'm sorry, I don't know your name."

"Anna Lucera. I'm his neighbor." She extended her hand. Jim took it and raised it to his lips theatrically.

"I'm Kevin Townsend, I don't think I told you, and this is Jim Thorpe. Would you like to join us?" Kevin stood up quickly, his bar stool scraping against the wooden floor.

"Oh, no, thank you. I'm here with my sister. She's

over there." Anna pointed to one of the tables at the far end of the room.

"Ask your sister to come over here too," Jim encouraged.

"We're just about to order, and we need to leave early because Lucia—she's my sister—has to be somewhere by eight-thirty, but thank you anyway."

"Good God!" Jim exclaimed as Anna walked away. "She's your neighbor?"

"That's what I said. I met her a few weeks ago. I didn't really meet her, it was more like I chased her down the hall and asked her about the plant on my balcony."

"Oh, good move, my friend. That'll get them every time." Jim laughed and reached up as if to give Kevin a high five.

Kevin and Jim sat at the bar for the next hour talking about the law firm and the cases they were working on, but Kevin couldn't dismiss his thoughts about Anna. He couldn't believe she had simply appeared at the same restaurant, and he started thinking about luck and timing and fate, and wondered whether he should have been more demonstrative towards her, but he had been caught off guard. The moment was over before he could get a handle on it. He decided he needed to track Anna down, and if that meant standing by the elevator door in their apartment building until he crossed paths with her again, then he would do it without hesitation.

At almost eight o'clock, Kevin left Max's. He stood out on the sidewalk, biding his time, watching people stroll down Canon Drive while he waited for the valet. He was in no rush, he had no plans for the night, and he liked taking in the sights of Beverly Hills.

"Yes, I am, I'm definitely going to be late, and I guarantee you it'll take forever to drive to Santa Monica in this traffic," Kevin overheard a woman say. He turned and found Anna standing with a woman who looked a little older but with similar features.

"I can always take a taxi back home. It's not that big of a deal. I promise I don't care."

Kevin seized the opportunity. "Excuse me, I couldn't help but overhear. It's close to eight o'clock right now, and if it would help you out, I could drive you home, Anna." He hoped his offer sounded casual.

The two sisters exchanged glances. "Is this the man you told me about?"

Anna shot her sister a hostile glance.

"It's all right, I'll get you there safely. I'm going home anyway."

"Well, if you wouldn't mind..." Anna moved closer to his side.

If Kevin could have jumped high enough, he would have jumped into the heavens and kissed his lucky stars.

Chapter Five

June 6, 1902
San Francisco

Anders Kristiansen could not believe his luck. He stood on the doorstep of the large Victorian house and collected himself before he knocked on the door. He straightened his tie, patted his breast-pocket handkerchief, knocked on the door, and waited. He wasn't sure whom he expected to answer the door, perhaps a butler from looking at the size of the house, but he was caught unprepared when the front door opened and there stood a startling, imposing figure dressed in an expensive three-piece suit.

"How kind of you to come. Do come in, I'm Domenico Sienna." The man held open the door.

"Anders Kristiansen, sir." Anders held out his hand and Domenico shook it firmly, looking him straight in the eyes.

"Yes, I know, we've been expecting you, Mr. Kristiansen. Right this way." Domenico closed the door and they walked across the entrance hall and into the drawing room.

Valeria's mother and another young woman sat facing each other on matching petit-point settees in the middle of the drawing room, while Valeria paced back and forth before the cut-glass window that faced the driveway. Valeria hurried towards him when her mother spoke loudly.

"Ah, Mr. Kristiansen, there you are, so good of you to come." Her mother glided elegantly towards him, holding out her hand, then quickly summoned over her shoulder, "Valeria, please come and greet our guest."

Valeria stepped over to Anders. "You received our note. I am so glad, Mr. Kristiansen."

"And I am equally as glad to have heard from you." Anders took Valeria's hand and looked down into her eyes.

"Can I pour you a cup of tea?"

"Yes, thank you." Anders paused. "I'm grateful to you," he said as she handed him the cup and saucer.

"Allow me to introduce my sister, Francesca." Valeria walked over to the other young woman and took her by the arm.

"I am charmed." Anders took Francesca's hand while she gave him a smile.

"I understand you're an artist, Mr. Kristiansen," Francesca said.

"I understand the same," Domenico said, taking over the conversation and settling into his winged-back chair like a king holding court.

"Yes, yes sir, I am." Anders looked from Francesca to Domenico. He didn't want to appear dismissive of Francesca but he knew to whom he should direct his answer. "I am a landscape painter as well as a portrait artist."

Domenico nodded his head and looked at Anders while Francesca seated herself next to Valeria on the divan before the fireplace.

"From Norway, I am told," Domenico continued.

"Yes sir, newly arrived in San Francisco," Anders

explained.

"And an acquaintance of Cornelia Davenworth," his host stated.

"Yes sir, Mrs. Davenworth is the niece of my mentor in Norway."

"Good, then, and what might his name be, Mrs. Davenworth's uncle who is also your mentor in Norway?" Domenico queried back while the rest of his family looked on as if watching a tennis match.

"A man by the name of Jorgensen, sir, Lars Jorgensen. It was he who encouraged me to come to San Francisco to paint the portrait of Mrs. Davenworth."

"We are all very fond of Mrs. Davenworth," Valeria's mother interjected. "Will you be staying on in San Francisco after your work is completed?"

"I will. I now have other work to keep me here after the portrait is completed. Mrs. Davenworth has been very generous with my introductions," Anders clarified.

Francesca smiled. "I would love to see your work."

"I would as well," Valeria joined in. "I hear you are very good at painting the portraits of women."

"Perhaps you have heard that because it is all anyone in San Francisco has seen me do." Anders looked at Valeria, who turned away, possibly gripped in a display of shyness.

Valeria couldn't believe he was here. He was so striking looking, all six-foot-three of lean masculinity which he carried with unselfconscious grace. He was beautiful, artistic-looking with his long blond hair framing the sharp planes of his face. There was something mesmerizing about his stormy blue eyes. They were the kind of disconcerting eyes that could look straight through a person as if they were under a spotlight, but for some reason she attributed his hypnotic gaze to self-confidence so it did not make her nervous.

Everything had happened so quickly. On a day like any other, she had agreed to accompany her mother to an art gallery in town, and that seemingly inconsequential act had left her feeling upside-down ever since. She didn't know how these things transpired. She wasn't prepared to feel this way. Never before in her life had she been so dramatically affected by anyone's presence, so she had absolutely nothing to compare when it came to this overwhelming emotion.

She felt entirely different about herself. Her senses exploded with life. She felt more aware of everything around her, and basked in the glowing light of happiness as she went about the most mundane of routines. She could not keep her thoughts off of Anders Kristiansen, and Valeria felt overpowered by the realization that Anders Kristiansen had abruptly manifested in her life and was pouring his attention all over her.

"It seems to be quite the fashion these days, the painting of portraits," her father observed. "You should be prosperous here, Mr. Kristiansen. It seems the subject matter for portraits ranges from the dearly departed to the family dog. Of one thing we can be certain in San Francisco, when one person of any repute does anything, there are a hundred people standing in line eager to do the same."

"Commemoration will always be in demand, sir. There is nothing new under the sun."

"No, I realize there is not." Domenico turned to Valeria. "It is Mr. Kristiansen's first visit here, Valeria.

Surely you must want him to see the garden that you and your sister take such joy in."

"Of course, Father." Valeria jumped to her feet. "It really is beautiful. It is just this way…if you are interested?"

"A thing of beauty is an endless fascination," Anders replied in a veiled compliment.

Valeria crossed the floor and went to the huge wrought-iron double doors that led from the drawing room out into the side garden.

Anders rose to join her. "With your permission, sir." Her father waved his hand dismissively and nodded his head.

They stepped outside onto the red brick walkway encasing the periphery of the house. Azalea bushes lined either side of the path and marigold, calla lilies, bougainvillea, and myriad other plants and flowers erupted everywhere. On each side of the house, a small clearing existed—complete with stone benches, wrought-iron chairs, and on the south side, a white polished-marble water fountain.

"Father knows a thing or two about commissioning work. He had this water fountain constructed out of Italian marble specifically for this area," Valeria volunteered.

Anders drew closer to the fountain, examining it thoughtfully. Valeria watched him as he did so and wondered what it was he was looking for. She considered the possibility that Anders, like most artists, understood an ephemeral quality that goes beyond what the eye merely beholds—a vision that encompasses movement with the recognition of style and the capacity to feel the intangible. She suspected she had a bit of the ability herself or she would not have been able to detect it in others.

"What do you think?" she asked Anders, who knelt down to touch the edge of the water basin.

"Come here, put your hands here, like this," he instructed. Valeria did as he asked. "What do you feel?" Anders glanced at her face.

"It feels cold."

"Yes? What else?"

"And it feels wet." She laughed out loud.

Anders laughed along with her, encouraging her further. "I know that. Now close your eyes and tell me what you feel from the stone—seriously, allow the images to come to you."

Valeria squeezed her eyes shut and concentrated. "Am I to use my imagination?"

"If you must, but it's easier to just let the images come to you."

Valeria let go of all expectations. She stretched the palms of her hands wide upon the stone and waited. She became aware of a slight tingling sensation, gently rippling throughout her entire body but focused upon the center of her chest. It left her warm, light, and joyous. Colors flitted before her eyes in shades of white and gold, although her lids remained closed. Suddenly, she realized she felt happy and her energy lifted.

"I almost want to dance!" She opened her eyes and smiled at Anders. "The simple pleasure I have from standing at this fountain fills me with something akin to satisfaction."

"As I expected," he said. "You are feeling the

emotions of the sculptor, which are embedded in the stone. Stone such as this retains emotional memory. In a way, there is a life to it."

"And the life here is the sculptor's emotional energy?"

"Yes. The sculptor's attitude towards his work, the emotions evoked as he created this work of art. All things receive and emit energy because anything of this earth has the ability to feel, even plants and stone," he responded softly.

"So what you are saying is the artist put the feeling of his joy for this creation into the stone…"

"And there it shall remain," Anders concluded her thought.

Valeria nodded in complete comprehension, because the truth of what he said resonated within her. She looked at Anders and reached out for his hand. Softly, she touched it and thought what a gentle man he must be. He wasn't like her loud, boisterous Italian cousins, or anything like her two brothers who were away at school in Italy. They could all fall face first into the fountain and never be able to feel the things Anders did. It seemed Anders recognized the awe and splendor in the mysterious world around them, and she thought those were admirable traits in a man.

She herself had always had a sense of the magical in life. Because she expected only good things to come her way from the arms of a benevolent universe, Valeria maintained a persistently optimistic attitude. Convinced all things worked together for good, she included her recent introduction to Anders Kristiansen within that concept. Fire touched her face at the bold move of touching his hand. Quickly, she removed it and backed away from the fountain.

Anders rose and captured Valeria's hand in his. He was not a man easily enthralled by women, but the one who stood before him captivated him completely. He looked in her dark brown eyes and studied their fathomless depths with intensity. He took in her long dark hair, almost black, and the way it lay in contrast against her porcelain-white skin. So small and delicate, yet there was something about her that made her appear bigger. She was regal, statuesque, and refined. She cast an impressive presence for one so diminutive, he thought.

"You are a beauty beyond compare." When she cast her eyes downward, he realized he had spoken out loud. "Please, don't let me frighten you, it is not my intention."

"My intention is to say the same of you."

"When I first saw you at the art gallery, I knew at once that I must know everything about you," Anders said. "I am prepared to do that, however long it takes, and you have all of my sincerity. You should know there is no other who holds my attention. I hope this is pleasing to you and not a worrisome inconvenience."

"It is not," Valeria assured him.

"It would be presumptuous of me to assume that I am the only one enamored of you," he tested.

"Perhaps, but it is a small community my family lives in," Valeria began. "We are meant to socialize with like-minded families and the individuals within them. Those with common histories, for example, those with common experiences and aspirations, as you can imagine."

"What I imagine is that you are talking about the Italian community."

"That is the truth of it, yes," Valeria affirmed.

"And as I am not of that lineage, would it be futile for me to continue on the path that I intend to pursue?"

"In my opinion, it would not be futile at all. If it pleases you and it pleases me, I see no harm."

"I am all too happy to hear that from you, but it is your father who concerns me," Anders confessed.

Valeria gathered her thoughts. The truth was she had no idea what her father would think. At the age of eighteen, she was inexperienced in the ways of courting because every young man who had kept her company had been in her life due to his affiliation with her family. There had been no intentional orchestration. They had simply been the children of her parents' friends, and she had grown up with most of them. She had never been interested, never encouraged, and had never thought of allowing momentum to gather with any of them. They were childhood playmates and nothing else.

Perhaps the implied understanding was when she did fall in love, it would have to be with an Italian, but she wasn't sure. She would have to bring the matter up with Francesca.

"I cannot speak for my father. It is not so easy to guess his mind on such things, but I do know that he loves me and truly wants the best for me. What makes me happy surely must be the best for me. I take great pride in saying that my father is not an unreasonable man."

"Well said." Anders smiled. "That being the case, then I will invest myself as I will, with your encouragement of course. I will simply address matters as they present themselves."

Valeria smiled, liking Anders' self-assured manner and hoping he considered her response to be an encouraging one. The light in her heart and the spring in her step as they walked back around the house and into the drawing room made her feel as if she glided upon air, and one look from Francesca as they entered the room told her everyone could see her emotions on display.

* * *

Later that night, she and Francesca sat by the fire in the upstairs sitting room. Her sister set aside her needlepoint. "Father said that Mr. Kristiansen is a noteworthy man."

"Noteworthy?" Valeria repeated. "Did he say anything else?"

"Of course he did. When does he ever leave well enough alone when it comes to either one of us?" Francesca laughed.

"Francesca, seriously, what else did he say?"

"I don't think he is impressed that Mr. Kristiansen is a painter. As you know, he considers painting to be a pleasant pastime for females but not one that is a lucrative career for a man."

"Well then, explain to me about the great Italian artists who hang their masterpieces throughout Europe!" Valeria retorted.

"I could explain that to you easily, but none of them are proposing to keep company with Domenico Sienna's daughter," Francesca replied. "Please, let's keep our voices down."

Valeria whispered, "What do you suppose this

means?"

"It means very little for now. I don't think Father has a sense for how you feel about this man. If what I perceive from you, according to what you've said so far, is correct, then there will be time enough for Father to ponder the full impact."

"Impact, indeed!" Valeria spoke more harshly than she intended. "Haven't we always been encouraged to follow our own hearts? Who would I be impacting other than myself?"

"Valeria, listen to reason. You know better than to ask such a question. Every move any of us makes impacts everyone within our family, and I know I don't have to explain anything further. None of us experiences anything alone. That's part of the glory and a little of the frustration of being in our family, but here we are."

"I did not mean to be harsh with you, Francesca. I am only frightened at the possibility Father will frown upon a relationship with a Norwegian man simply for his crime of being Norwegian."

"With good reason, Valeria. Father's only certainty is with his Italian heritage. It is his stability and it helps him define who he is. Italy has the only culture he believes in and therefore trusts. Even though he is in America and he loves it, he still clings to the old ways, as he likes to call them. In case you have not noticed, Father has managed to create an Italian culture right here in San Francisco. Just look at his business associates and all of his close friends. It is not so unusual. Many other cultures cling together in a similar way. It is all about familiarity and common social morals. What he wants to give his children is a safe journey through life. He means no harm beyond his understanding, but I believe we will have to be patient with him," Francesca soothed.

"But Father is so open-minded."

"Yes, I agree. He is open-minded in the respect of being a good listener, and he takes the time to ponder others' vantage points, but this is different. Father is a progressive thinker with regard to his attitude towards women—this is one of the reasons he is so lenient when it comes to any of us following our own interests. It is also why you and I went to a private girls' school. It's not every parent who sees the merit in educating a girl child. That being said, the subject of who to take seriously as a suitor falls into a different category, because the man will have to fit into our family. Do you see the difference? Now tell me, when is Mr. Kristiansen to call upon you again?"

"Let's call him Anders," Valeria decided. "He wants to call upon me the day after tomorrow and take me to his studio. He hopes you can accompany me as a chaperone."

"I will, of course," Francesca obliged, "though we cannot simply make plans on our own. We are going to have to present this to Mother, who will present the subject to Father for his approval, and we're going to have to instigate this as soon as possible because Father always needs time to consider. Do not forget, we have to be patient with Father. What time does Anders wish us to arrive? I assume it will be in the afternoon after your ballet class."

"Yes, we are invited for four o'clock tea. He will come to collect us."

"Then we will talk to Mother first thing in the

morning. Remember, we need to be patient with Father."

"Yes, I will be especially patient. Oh Francesca, thank you for talking to me. I do adore you." Valeria walked over to her sister and gave her a warm hug.

"You would do the same for me."

"I would, and more. I would stop the tide of the sea for you if you needed it," Valeria said with conviction.

Chapter Six

June, 1998 – February, 1999
Los Angeles

Kevin opened the passenger door of his Jeep Cherokee and cautioned Anna to watch her step. He closed the door behind her and walked around to the driver's seat. Swinging inside, he fastened his seatbelt and merged into the traffic of a Thursday night in Beverly Hills. Acutely aware of Anna sitting beside him, he wanted to do everything correctly, including driving cautiously, just in case she watched him.

After parking in the underground lot beneath the apartment building, he walked around to the passenger side and chivalrously opened the door.

"It is such a small world," Kevin began, suddenly aware of his nervousness. He couldn't get over how beautiful she was.

"It really is, but I am so glad it is," she responded. When the elevator door opened, Anna stepped in and pressed the number six. "I can't tell you how nice it is to run into you again. I was hoping I would, and thank you so much for offering me a ride home. You really helped me and Lucia tonight."

"Glad to do it, any time," he responded, feeling flattered. He waited in a pregnant pause, wondering how to prolong the moment, as the elevator door opened. "Um, I don't know if you have plans for the rest of the night, but if you'd like some company…I mean, I would like that, and, um, if you wanted to come and look at my plant, it's just out on the balcony and—"

"I'd love to," Anna said as they stepped into the hall.

"Great! All right. I'm just this way." He turned left and led her towards his apartment. He shook his head slightly to clear it. He wasn't usually nervous around women. He was the kind of guy who had to fight women off more often than not, but this was different. Anna was different, and he could see it right away.

He unlocked the door, and Anna sailed into the room as if she'd been there many times before. He found himself following her as she walked straight to the balcony, waiting for him to unlock the sliding glass door.

"Now then, let's have a look at your plant. Have you been talking to it?" She leaned over and put her hand to one of its leaves.

"Yes, every day. I've been asking it to do me the favor of living. I wouldn't want its death on my hands, you know."

"Of course not, that would be bad karma." She smiled. "It looks healthy and thriving to me." She turned to face him.

"Thanks to you." Kevin smiled back. "I did invest in a water purifier. It's in the kitchen, so I did follow your advice. How do you know so much about plants?" he asked, genuinely curious. He wanted to know everything about her and this was a good beginning.

"I don't really know a lot about them, but my sister does. You should see Lucia's apartment, it's like a greenhouse. She should be a professional botanist. She knows the name of every plant and how to tend to its needs. I've picked up a little from Lucia, but mostly I just have a natural way with them."

"So you were born with this talent?" Kevin wanted to know more.

She laughed. "With a few more talents than just a natural way with plants!"

Kevin kept the momentum going. "Oh, yeah? Like what else?"

"Let me think about this. Okay I'm not bad at dancing," Anna volunteered.

Kevin could just picture her in motion; she was so lithe and graceful from what he could tell. He wondered if she meant dancing as in going out to clubs and dancing for fun, or if dancing was something she took seriously and studied.

"What kind of dancing do you mean?"

"I take ballet classes. I'm one of those people who started young and never put it down. I just came to ballet naturally when I was a little girl. It was like I was born knowing how to do it. I still take classes twice a week. I like any kind of movement, like vinyasa flow yoga, and sometimes Pilates—even though it's kind of boring but I do it anyway. I just like to keep moving."

"So dancing is like a sport for you," Kevin summarized.

"That's a good way to put it. I think that's it!"

"That's two talents you have. What else?"

"I'm a pretty good painter, and I'm good with animals."

"Painting? My mother's a painter. What kind of painting are we talking about?"

"Watercolors mostly. Believe me, what I do is small scale painting," Anna explained. "I only do it for enjoyment."

"As coincidence would have it, so do I," Kevin confessed.

"But that's not what you do for a living, right? I've noticed you don't dress the part." Anna grinned at him.

"Good eye you've got." He pulled out a balcony chair for her and settled himself on another one. "I'm a lawyer, but I'd be a painter if I thought I could make a living at it. I think the love of painting is just in my blood. My mother actually does make a living at it, so I grew up having it around me. With painting, I'm probably the way you are with dancing. Some talents we're just born with."

"I agree. It's a question of what you decide to develop. Anyway, it sounds like you have a real job."

"I do. And you?"

"Oh, I have a real job, but not as real as yours," she teased.

"All right, confess. What do you do?"

"I'm a freelance writer, thank God. I don't have to do the nine-to-five thing in anybody's office, which means that my time is my own if I can just find the discipline."

"And do you find the discipline?"

"Yes, definitely. My motivation is to avoid office drama at all costs. I think about that whenever I'm tempted to get lazy."

"Is writing the lesser of all evils or do you really enjoy it?"

"I really enjoy it, seriously. It took me quite a few years to be able to freelance for a living."

"You don't look old enough to have that many years behind you. How old are you?"

"How old do you think I am?" she asked.

This is a loaded gun, he thought. "Twenty," he said, wanting to be on the safe side.

"Yeah, right." She narrowed her eyes at him. "I'm twenty-six. Now it's your turn. How old are you?"

"I'm an old man, over the hill completely."

"The hill, of course, being thirty?"

"You got it." Kevin smiled.

"*Over* the hill or *on* it?" she specified.

"On it." He watched for her response. He realized what he wanted more than anything was to simply look at her. Anna had so many interesting qualities, he wanted to break them all down and study her piece by piece. First, her size and the way she moved. Small, lithe, and graceful as a ballerina, yet at the same time she moved with athletic certainty. She carried herself with confidence and total awareness of her body's strength and agility. Five-feet-five and slender, with long, heavy, dark hair and light green eyes. Her hair was the darkest he had ever seen for somebody with such fair skin. *Lucera,* he thought to himself, *Italian, isn't it?*

"Thirty really isn't so old," she continued. "Not in the grand scheme of things, anyway. It depends on what you've done with your life up until thirty and where you plan on going from there. Obviously you've done more than sit around, if you're a lawyer."

Kevin laughed. "You're right about that."

"Where do you work now? What law firm?"

"Williams and Khan in Century City."

"Do you like your work?"

"So far, I do. It's the second firm I've worked for since I graduated from law school. The first one was in

Boston. Johnson and Wexler. They were entertainment attorneys, and it led me to Los Angeles because the firm constantly interacted with lawyers out here."

"Yeah, well, I can see that. If you're involved in the entertainment industry in any way, sooner or later it leads to either New York or L.A."

"That's right, this is where it all happens first," Kevin agreed.

* * *

It was amazingly easy to talk to Anna, Kevin thought later that evening. She was unpretentious, unguarded, and nonjudgmental. He liked her confidence and easy-going manner. She was humorous, smart, and well-informed. Eleven o'clock, when she said she had to leave, came way too soon. He wanted to see her again as soon as possible.

On Saturday mornings at ten, she said, she attended a yoga class in West Hollywood, and if he was game, they could go together. He almost said no way, he wasn't interested—but changed his mind. He wanted to seize any opportunity to be with her, so he feigned enthusiasm instead.

* * *

Their attendance at the Saturday morning yoga class was what Kevin considered to be the start of their relationship, and it turned into a steady progression from there. Over the following eight months, Kevin took her to restaurants, and she took him to the theater. They explored art galleries together and hiked the trails through the Santa Monica Mountains. They spent weekend afternoons at the beaches in Malibu and made frequent outings to places like Ventura, Santa Barbara,

San Luis Obispo, and a few overnight stays in Carmel. He met all of Anna's friends, and she eventually met his parents when they came to visit from Massachusetts.

Each time he saw her, Kevin fell more deeply in love. They were uncannily well-suited, Kevin reflected, because they balanced each other. They were similar in background, upbringing, and education, but they differed in areas such as temperament and the subject of religion.

Kevin was level-headed, even-keeled, and saw the world in a way that tended to be black and white. In contrast, Anna was whimsical, capricious, and fascinated in subjects that touched upon the arcane sciences. She told him she wasn't religious, but instead spiritual. She was a voracious reader and dived into subjects that ranged from past life regression to spirits from the "other side."

In her living room, a bookcase held pride of place with books from authors such as Caroline Myss, Marianne Williamson, John Holland, James Redfield, and Barbara Ann Brennan. She would bring her current reading material to Kevin and read excerpts to him that resonated with her. Anna understood a language whose foundation was intuitive and ephemeral. She didn't want to be schooled, she had said to Kevin; it was more that she wanted to know what like minds were thinking. She explained it helped her to synthesize her own understanding of life's purpose and the journey of the soul.

Deep within her, Anna had a natural relationship with the mystical, and exploring the manifestations of it intrigued her no end. She would read aloud from her books, add her comments, and Kevin would raise a skeptical eyebrow and ask her for proof. They would debate various subjects, and although one would assume Kevin was the stronger debater, he was no match for Anna—she held her beliefs so firmly in hand.

"Oh ye of little faith." Anna laughed at Kevin, but she never tried to convince or convert. She came from a very specific premise in life, and it entailed her belief that life is an ongoing mystery. Anna planned on getting to the bottom of it.

"Let me know when you have it all figured out. I'll be at the law office," Kevin had joked one morning as he got ready to go to work—for as time developed, their individual apartments became common ground though they spent most of their time in Kevin's.

He returned after six that night to find Anna hunched over an easel she had set up in the corner of the kitchen.

"Ah, the artist at work," he observed. "What is it you're creating now?"

"I can't tell you until it's finished, so don't sneak over here and look. I'm making you a present," Anna warned, but he heard the joy in her voice.

"What in the world did I do to deserve this?" Kevin asked, thinking *this is the kind of thing I like about her the best: I never know what I'm going to walk in to.*

"Nothing short of bringing the stars out in the night to shine down upon me, that's all." Anna straightened up and walked towards him.

"You have paint all over you. Look at your shirt." Kevin drew back and took off his coat.

"The better to greet you with, my dear." She pulled

her workshirt off and reached her arms out towards him.

"Now this is the way to greet your man at the end of a hard workday." Kevin stepped into her arms and held her close. He ran his hands down her back and kissed her warmly.

Anna laughed. "If you give me just a couple of minutes I'll be finished, so don't get carried away just yet."

"All right, I'll let you go, but only if you keep your shirt off so I can stare at you."

"Sorry, but I work better with it on." Anna laughed again and walked back to her easel, pulling her shirt over her head. She narrowed her eyes and assessed the canvas one last time. "I talked to Lucia a little while ago," she called into the living room, where Kevin sat going through the mail.

"Are you finished yet?" Kevin returned.

"No. Stay where you are. I need to make sure it's ready," Anna instructed.

"How is Lucia?"

"She's great, as usual. Would you like to meet her for dinner in a little while?"

"What time?"

"Eight o'clock at Atlantic?"

"That's West Hollywood, isn't it?" Kevin recalled.

"Yes, what do you think?"

"Okay. I'm going to jump in the shower and change my clothes."

"Wait for me," Anna called, resting her paintbrush on the easel and following him into the bathroom.

"We're not going to get anything accomplished with both of us in here. I thought you were still painting."

"Oh yes we are, we're going to get a *lot* accomplished. And by the way, I've decided I'm finished with your present. Anyway, you started it."

"I started it? You take your shirt off the second I step through the door and I started it?"

"Yes, you started it when you walked through the door."

"Come here." Kevin drew her into the shower with him.

A bit later, they emerged from the shower soaked and happy, for theirs was a connection that went beyond either of their imaginations. It was deeper than longing or desire—it felt as if they had commingled souls that melded into one. An almost desperate familiarity existed and both of them were acutely aware they were perfect for each other.

Kevin watched Anna as she reached for a towel. "I feel like I've known you my entire life."

"Maybe you have," she responded quickly. "Maybe we've been together before and are doing this all over again."

"What, loving each other?" Kevin wanted to know.

"Yes, again," Anna said simply. She draped herself in a white oversized towel and began to walk into the living room. "Are you coming?"

"I'm right behind you."

Anna stood to one side of the easel, making room for Kevin. "I'm ready to show this to you now."

Kevin stood to the left of Anna and stared at the painting. In bold colors of red, blue, and green, with flecks of gold throughout, a semi-transparent star hung suspended in the middle of the canvas.

"This is what you are to me. You've brought the stars from the sky to shine down upon me."

Chapter Seven

June 8, 1902
San Francisco

"Valeria!" Francesca called for the third time. "We haven't got all day. Mr. Kristiansen will be arriving within the hour to collect us. Where are you?"

Valeria appeared in Francesca's bedchamber. "I've been in Mother's room. I hope you don't mind, but she wants to talk to the two of us at the same time."

"Concerning what? It appears you've already been talking to her. Might I ask what this is about?" Francesca returned.

"She wants to ensure that we both behave ourselves properly."

Francesca sent her a knowing glance. "We've been over this a dozen times, but be that as it may, we'll go to her now." She walked to the door. Valeria followed directly behind her, and they crossed through the sitting room and down the long hallway leading to their mother's room.

"Oh good, the two of you. Let's have a seat, shall we?" Adriana glided across her bedroom floor and settled onto the chaise lounge that occupied the central position of a seating arrangement before the large bay window overlooking the garden below. A vase of freshly cut hydrangea graced the round footed table standing between the two upholstered chairs where Valeria and Francesca took a seat.

"Francesca," their mother began, "I am confident Valeria is in the best of care with you as her chaperone this afternoon."

"I most certainly am," Valeria offered, though she ceased to continue as her mother shot her a silencing look. She turned to look at Francesca, who sat demurely waiting for their mother's instructions.

"No doubt this afternoon you girls will conduct yourselves as you've always done in the past, with subtlety, discretion, and perfect comportment. I understand you will be taking afternoon tea, and I do not have to remind you that after a sufficiently appropriate length of time it becomes rude to linger. Francesca, I know you will be sensitive to the length of time."

"Of course I will, Mother," Francesca complied.

"Certainly it will be well before dark, so I needn't worry the two of you will be out past daylight."

"Absolutely not, Mother, I will see to it," Francesca confirmed.

"I trust that I needn't remind you it is utterly inappropriate to leave your sister unchaperoned for even the slightest moment."

"I wouldn't dream of it," Francesca assured.

Adriana looked towards the bronze crystal-faced clock that sat on her bedside table. "What time does Mr. Kristiansen's carriage arrive?"

"Three o'clock, Mother," Valeria answered.

"You'll need to ready yourselves." She looked at Valeria. "I should think that your new white cotton high-necked blouse and a suitable skirt with a petticoat or two should wear nicely."

"Oh, Mother," Valeria protested, "the fashion now

leans towards a more close-fitting skirt, and few ladies are wearing petticoats these days!"

"Yes, I realize times are changing and with them the fashions. I am also aware of what our dressmaker has dreamed up for you, but I will have a good look at you before you leave, is that understood?"

"Yes, thank you." Valeria dismissed herself. She strode back to her room leaving Francesca behind to seal things with their mother. When Francesca joined her, Valeria was already dressed.

"Is this appropriate?" Valeria turned in her new-fashioned skirt. "What do you think?"

"I think you should pin your white gold brooch at your neck and wear no other jewelry," Francesca offered, "but yes, you look lovely. Your new skirt is very flattering. Run and show Mother and I'll be with you in a moment."

After procuring her mother's approval, who cautioned Valeria to be mindful of her propensity to chatter too much and also reminding her that men liked to take the lead in conversations, Valeria waited in the entrance hall for Francesca with only ten minutes to spare before the arrival of Anders Kristiansen's carriage.

"We must not be standing here in the entrance hall when the carriage arrives," Francesca admonished as she descended the stairs. "Come with me into the drawing room and we'll wait there."

Valeria followed closely. "What difference could it possibly make where we wait?"

"It is a difference of appearances. One must not appear too eager, after all."

"But Francesca, I *am* eager!" Valeria exclaimed.

"I know you are, Valeria, but you must learn how to fulfill your role and let Mr. Kristiansen fulfill his as well."

"Mother says I have perfect manners," Valeria protested.

"Of course you do, but you are new in the ways of courting and that is an entirely different matter." Francesca held firm.

"So I shouldn't appear too eager and I am to pretend indifference?" Valeria interpreted.

"Well, there is something to be said for encouragement, Valeria, but what I'm suggesting is merely that you let Mr. Kristiansen—"

"Anders," Valeria interjected.

"*Mr. Kristiansen* to his face until he asks us otherwise. Oh, you are exasperating!"

"What were you saying before that?" Valeria continued.

"Mr. Kristiansen's role is to come to you, and your role is to let him," Francesca concluded.

Valeria went to the drawing room window and looked out towards the driveway. Mr. Kristiansen's carriage turned through the wrought-iron gates separating the driveway from the main road.

"He's here!" she gasped.

"Then get away from the window and we'll let Sergio answer the door."

"Mother!" Valeria called.

"Yes, yes, I know," her mother answered, sweeping gracefully into the intricately designed drawing room. "Come now, quickly, let me hug you both goodbye and wish you a happy afternoon. Remember what we have discussed. I'll be expecting you back before the sun sets."

"We'll come to you the moment we return," Francesca said as a chime sounded overhead announcing the arrival of Anders.

Moments later, he appeared in the doorway of the drawing room preceded by Sergio the butler, who spoke directly to their mother. "Mr. Kristiansen, ma'am."

Valeria as well as her sister and mother smiled.

"Once again, I am charmed, ladies." Anders bowed. "Mrs. Sienna, I hope you can part with your two lovely daughters for this one afternoon?"

"I can indeed, Mr. Kristiansen. I understand you will be taking them to tea at your art studio."

"I will. It is a humble place but perhaps informative for the likes of two art enthusiasts." He smiled.

"Well, then, don't let me keep you." She led the way into the entrance hall.

The carriage, although not an ornate one, had plenty of room. A formal coachman made a big display of lowering a step and ushering Valeria and Francesca inside. Anders seated himself across from them, and they began the fifteen-minute journey to the home of Mrs. Davenworth.

* * *

"I will now give you ladies the brief tour," Anders offered upon their arrival. He took off his hat and placed it on the table beside the front door of the carriage house he rented from Mrs. Davenworth.

"How lovely!" enthused Valeria, taking in the work space all at once.

"How quaint and charming," Francesca joined in.

"It is none of those, but I thank you just the same." Anders laughed. "This is a functional place that holds little in the way of distraction, which after all is the entire point."

"Can we see what you're working on?" Valeria waved toward three freestanding easels positioned in the middle of the room.

"I'd be happy to show you. I currently have three paintings in the works. Two are by commission and one I am doing for pleasure."

The girls followed Anders as he made his way to the first canvas. The portrait in progress bore a striking resemblance to Mrs. Davenworth but without her physical flaws. She wore a long-sleeved teal-colored dress fitted tightly from her neck to her waist then buffeting out to her ankles. She stood against an oval mist-like backdrop, wearing a wide-brimmed cream-colored hat and wielding a matching parasol angled a pace before her.

"I would know this woman anywhere. It is beautiful and much to her likeness," Francesca volunteered.

"My deepest gratitude, Miss Sienna," Anders said humbly.

"Mr. Kristiansen, has Mrs. Davenworth seen this yet? I know if she has, she must be pleased," Valeria said.

"She has not, but soon enough she will. I followed the advice of my mentor in Norway who thinks it best to show the portrait only after it is completed, Miss Sienna. This way, it removes the temptation for the subject to offer any critique." Anders looked at Valeria, and she could have sworn he winked at her. "I would be eternally grateful if you would call me by my Christian name," he added.

Valeria shot an inquisitive look at Francesca, who

nodded almost imperceptibly.

"Thank you, Anders, and we would be grateful for you to call us by our given names as well," replied Valeria.

"Well, that settles things, does it not?" He walked over to the second canvas. "This one is not typical of what I have painted in the past, so I find the process to be a refreshing challenge. The subject is the nine-year-old son of an acquaintance of Mrs. Davenworth. He is a well enough behaved little boy, but he finds it extremely challenging to sit still for any length of time. I suspect this one will take longer to complete than any I've done previously."

Francesca drew closer to the canvas, commenting on the color of the young boy's eyes.

"They are actually a paler version than this blue that you see here, but because of the sailor suit he wears, the color is intensified," Anders explained. "His mother prefers to dress him in that style as he is far too young for a waistcoat and trousers."

As Anders and Francesca studied the painting, Valeria crept around to the third of Anders' works in progress. She stood still and, with wide eyes, sharply drew in a breath that escaped in a gasp. "Anders," she called over to him, "where is this?"

"That, Valeria, is a favorite place of mine not too far from here. It is south of San Francisco, about four and a half hours by train, in an area that is only recently settled. It is called Carmel and it lies on the Monterey Peninsula."

"The colors in the ocean are breathtaking!" Valeria exclaimed. "Are the colors truly so brilliant? This is absolutely beautiful."

Francesca stood by Valeria's side and looked at the canvas. "Arresting colors. You are very talented, Anders. This painting is remarkably inviting. It makes me want to wade right into the water, which would be folly as I hardly know how to swim. I have such a sense of foreboding when it comes to water, but looking at your painting makes me want to forget all that and jump right in."

"Thank you, Francesca. My only hope is that I have justified the actual beauty. There are truly colors in the sea that challenge my best efforts at interpretation. The water along the coast of Carmel has an iridescent quality, with spectrums of blues and greens that can only be found in nature. Because of the massive rocks lining the coast, there are always white-capped waves moving inland, sometimes hitting the rocks and spraying upwards so the water seems to be in constant motion. It is therefore hard to capture because it is constantly changing." Anders stood looking down, considering his own work.

"What are these trees here?" Valeria pointed at the canvas.

"Cypress trees. They grow all throughout the Monterey Peninsula. Unusual, aren't they?"

"Magnificent. Look how their trunks twist and turn, and their tops look like green featherbeds. Francesca, have you ever heard of Carmel?"

"I never have." Francesca peered closer at the canvas. "So, this is the painting you are doing for pleasure?" She turned to Anders, who nodded his head.

"Yes, it is *sheer* pleasure. It is ultimately a practice towards wish fulfillment. I dream of one day living there."

"I like it better than the others," Valeria stated.

"I am certain Valeria means they are all splendid, Anders," Francesca explained.

Anders smiled a broad grin that told Valeria he knew exactly what she meant.

"It looks like a magical place," she enthused. "What else can you tell us about Carmel?"

"I received word, when I first came to California, that a coastal area was in development by a group of writers and artists just south of San Francisco. Intrigued, and encouraged by the news of recently laid train tracks, I went to see it for myself. This painting is of Carmel Bay, which lies like an arc at the bottom of the town. The bay's beauty surpasses anything I have ever seen. There are massive white sand dunes that flow down to the water's edge, then the beach stretches for almost a mile in either direction. It is an untouched cove lined by cypress trees and is a favorite location among the locals.

"The weather changes dramatically from hour to hour, yet the locals are always there—walking along the beach or laying a picnic. Many do as I was drawn to do and bring an easel and paint. The bay is absolutely inspirational. In fact, it is quite mystical."

Anders moved towards the open kitchen and set a kettle of water to boil for the tea. He returned with a tray of scones and two different kinds of jam, along with clotted cream and fresh strawberries.

"Landscapes are a new pursuit of mine, but I find my interest in them grows with each endeavor," he continued. "Working with watercolors helps me to capture the translucency of the sea with better accuracy.

It is something I am exploring right now."

Valeria and Francesca seated themselves on either side of Anders, upon a high-back petit-point sofa with a footed rectangular coffee table before it. As the rules of civility dictated, they had their tea promptly at four o'clock and talked idly of amusing things. The sound of a dog barking sailed through the open window. Francesca leapt to her feet, asking where the sound came from.

"My dog and faithful companion, Greta," Anders answered. "Unusual enough for a Norwegian, she is a German shepherd. She is only twelve weeks old or I would have her in here with us. Unfortunately, she is still learning her manners and cannot be trusted around two young ladies. I suspect if she were in here, she would scramble all over your pretty clothes and nip at your heels in the process."

"Then I must go and see her," Francesca returned. "You don't mind, do you?"

Valeria and Anders exchanged a look that told them both they would relish the opportunity to be alone together for a brief moment. Anders stood up and offered Francesca an open door.

"I'll help you clear away your tea service," Valeria offered. She felt excited, she felt nervous—self-conscious and extremely aware that this one moment could be the highlight of her life thus far. Something so seemingly inconsequential as being alone with Anders Kristiansen for the second time was pivotal to her, and she wanted to be present in the moment, conduct herself appropriately, charm him, enamor him, verify his suspicions that she was, in fact, worth pursuing. She wanted to see it in his eyes—wanted to hear a word, any word that would let her know he felt the same.

Anders' light touch on her wrist stopped her from clearing the tea service. "I wouldn't have you lift a finger. It is my pleasure to serve you. Each time I am in your company, all I can think of is when I'll be granted permission to do so again."

"You flatter me," Valeria whispered softly, though she had the courage to meet his eyes.

"Do you remember when we knelt before the stone of the water fountain in your garden?"

Valeria nodded, listening to him, studying him.

"Do you remember my asking you to try your best and feel the energy of the stone?" Anders took her hand firmly in his.

"I do remember, and I did, of course, feel the stone's energy."

"I know you did, Valeria. I ask you this because I want to say that when I take your hand in mine, an extraordinary energy runs through me, leaving me more alive. I have been waiting for this current my entire life."

Words caught in her throat, because she too felt an electrical charge when she held Anders' hand. She told herself she must say something in response, and that particular something must express encouragement.

"I can feel it as well," she confessed. "I like it when you take my hand."

"One can feel so much through the hands." Anders closed both of his hands around hers and looked down as if to study the effect.

"Our hands fit together nicely." Valeria looked up at him.

"*We*, my dear, fit together nicely," Anders agreed.

The door opened and Francesca averted her gaze as she entered the room. Valeria turned quickly towards her. "I have been telling Anders that Mother and Father are having a croquet party this Sunday and how lovely it would be to have him join us."

Although Valeria had made no mention of a party, thankfully Anders followed her lead. "It would be my pleasure. And now, ladies, allow me to see you safely to your home." Anders offered Valeria his arm.

Chapter Eight

March 11, 1999
Los Angeles

"No, no, lie down and keep still. You don't have to take your shirt off."

Anna directed Kevin to a navy-blue massage table she had recently purchased and set up in the middle of the living room. Her black cat leaped up onto the table.

"Come on, Franny, get down." Anna lifted her cat gently and set her softly on the floor.

"This cat is everywhere, isn't she? She always has to be in the middle of things."

"Cats go where the love is," Anna pointed out. "It's a good sign, and Franny is a good judge of character. She's my protector. Believe me, if Franny didn't like you I'd have serious reservations about you as well."

"Whatever you say, but I don't understand what I'm supposed to be doing."

"You're not supposed to be *doing* anything except lying quietly, face up," Anna calmly instructed.

"Tell me what you're doing again?" Kevin lay down with a dramatic exhale.

"I'm going to read your auric field."

"With what?" He turned his head and looked over at her.

"With my hands. I'm gathering information." Anna approached the table. "My hands are sensitive. I can feel things with them. Most people can if they're paying attention."

"Wait a minute." Kevin sat up and dangled his legs over the side of the table. "Explain to me how this works."

"Well, it's an intuitive art, first of all. This is what I've been studying for the past year in the class I've been taking that meets once a month in Venice. I've told you about it but only cryptically. I'm learning how to read people's energy fields."

"I understand that part, but I don't really understand *how* you're doing it."

"It's easier to show you, but I can give you a little bit of an explanation."

"That would be good. Then I'll be able to figure out what I'm supposed to be doing."

"You're not supposed to *do* anything," Anna said again. "Okay, so here's how it works: There is an energy field—some call it an auric field—that surrounds each of us, comprised of seven layers. Each of these layers corresponds to one of the seven energy centers within the body. These energy centers are also known as chakras, and they are actually the channels through which we give and receive, or rather process, information."

"Information from where?"

"From everything around us. Every living thing gives off energy. Think about it. We're all capable of receiving impressions beyond our five senses. I'll give you an example. Have you ever noticed how you can be subtly affected by someone close to you who is in a bad mood? They might not be saying or doing anything to let you know they're in a bad mood, but somehow you're aware of it. Or if you've ever been the recipient of someone's anger, it's usually a lot more than words being thrown at you. It's the energy. It's a little difficult to explain because I'm not convinced we have an adequate language to explain what I'm talking about."

"All right, I agree. We're all affected by each other's moods, I'll give you that." Kevin nodded.

"Good. Now, you have to ask yourself, where does that energy being directed at you go?"

"Into thin air, I guess."

"In a best case scenario, that can be part of it, but what is typical is for that energy to take up residency in your auric field. That's only part of it though. Your own thoughts and emotions emanate into your auric field as well. They also affect your chakras for better or worse."

Kevin looked puzzled. "So you're going to read my energy field with your hands?"

"Exactly. I want to see what's there and how it affects your chakras," Anna explained, somewhat relieved he was beginning to understand.

"Well, if something *is* there, what can you do about it?"

"I can help to facilitate a clearer auric field primarily by addressing the individual chakras, but first I have to take a look at what's there."

"Interesting." Kevin swung his legs back onto the table and lay down.

"It is extremely interesting. Again, I work with my hands. There are only three other people in the class I'm taking. Two of them work visually to obtain the same information I look for, and by that I mean they can stand across the room from someone and be able to 'see' what's going on."

"In the auric field," Kevin added.

"Yes. Keep in mind that it's an intuitive art."

"Then you ought to be good at this." Kevin thought of the numerous times Anna had called him the second he was thinking of her, how often she finished his sentences when they were half-way out of his mouth, how she could verbalize a suggestion he had not yet fully formed, and more often than not how she effortlessly read his mind. "Okay," he threw in the proverbial towel, "let's get started."

Anna stepped to the massage table and hovered over Kevin, her hands stretched out over his body, her eyes closed, with an intent look upon her face as if she were listening for something. She drew her hands up into the air above him and slowly began to ease them downward. They stopped a foot above him. She drew them up again and brought them back down to the same point. It was as if an invisible wall precluded her from going beyond that particular spot, so she stepped to the top of the table and made a sweep of the air with her graceful hands from his head to his toes. She repeated the movement twice, then stopped and placed her hands directly above his solar plexus.

"What are you finding?" Kevin asked.

"I'm looking at your third chakra."

"Why?"

"Because there seems to be some stagnation there."

"Meaning what?"

"The third chakra relates to one's sense of self. I'm going to clear out the stagnation and take it from there. I know once I do, there will be further information."

"Do you want me to be quiet?" Kevin whispered.

"That would be a good thing for now. Just let me keep going," Anna whispered back.

Anna drew her hands up again—there seemed to be another wall high up in the air. Again, she made a sweep of his body from that level and resumed her stance of active listening. Drawing her hands up a fourth time, she moved them as if they were being led involuntarily to a point six inches below where they were previously. She made another sweep from that point and placed her hands directly over Kevin's forehead. Leaning closely over the area, Anna lightly tapped the point between his eyebrows.

"Can you just let your breath out now, like a big exhale?" Anna instructed.

Kevin followed the instruction and let his breath out loudly.

"Good, let me see... Okay, this is what I'm getting." She shook her head, as if doing so would help her to synthesize the information into a cohesive picture. "There's an issue with your sense of self, with the way you see or perceive yourself. It's an issue of identity, and I discovered that from your third chakra. Then when I found activity in your seventh auric layer, I knew it tied in with your third chakra in a way that implied there is higher meaning to the issue. It indicates there is a spiritual lesson at hand. There is definitely something here for you to learn. Then I found activity in your sixth auric layer, so I took a closer look at your sixth chakra."

"What's the sixth chakra? Is that like the sixth sense?"

"Pretty close. I'm impressed." Anna smiled down at him. "The sixth chakra relates to what is called the third eye, which is considered the seat of intuition. It also relates to the memory of learned wisdom, past and present, so to speak."

"Past? You mean like past lives?"

"Very likely, yes. I'm getting very clear information. I think if I were to spell it out succinctly, I would have to say that what's in your field is an issue of remembering who you are from a spiritual perspective."

"That's all?"

"That's a *lot*. Any time you get higher information, it is a big deal. Not everybody carries that kind of thing around with them, believe me."

Kevin sat up and looked at Anna, opening his mouth then closing it. Finally, he decided to move on to a topic that didn't focus on him. "So do you plan on doing more of this work, like for other people?"

"I haven't thought that far ahead. I've only been fine-tuning my understanding of the process and finding out something about my abilities. I mean, you don't know what you've got in the way of intuitive skills until you put them to practice, you know?"

"I guess you're right." He moved off the table. Carefully, he began to fold in the legs of the table and buckle the sides. "God help me, I'm married to a witch," he muttered under his breath.

"You're what?" Anna proclaimed loudly. "I am not a witch, I'm simply working on heightening my intuitive abilities. And by the way, nobody around here is married!"

"We could be," Kevin said softly. "We should be."

Chapter Nine

June 14, 1902
San Francisco

A feeling of expectation wafted throughout the Sienna house and drifted out into the front yard where five hired men clustered together in their common pursuit of assembling a large white canvas marquee tent. Three other workers in shifts carried a total of thirty-four chairs from the cellar of the house to the front garden, which offered a clear view of the unobstructed lawn where two croquet courses were set up.

Inside, servants assembled serving trays of cucumber sandwiches, assorted vegetable platters, fruit trays, pastries, roasted nuts, and large pitchers of iced tea and lemonade—all of which would be moved outside. The guests had been invited for two o'clock and it was a moderately temperate San Franciscan Sunday.

Adriana Sienna surveyed the activity from beneath her new wide-brimmed custom-made hat and was pleased. She always thought that croquet was the perfect vehicle for entertaining a large number of guests—particularly suitable for women since it required considerable skill but not too much strength or technique. Although croquet was not particularly popular with men, it did have both social and economic advantages. Men and women could play together and it required little equipment and no special clothing. In Adriana's line of thinking, if one gave one's guests a game to play, they could entertain themselves.

Adriana was a lucky woman in so many ways, most of all by having a husband who obliged her when it came to entertaining. Domenico had a hands-off policy culled from the belief that entertaining was woman's domain and best left in their capable hands. The only thing he required was for his wife to tell him where and when to appear, for he took immeasurable pride in her social orchestrations. He liked the fact that she handled everything to the last detail and reveled in the knowledge that she instructed her two daughters meticulously on the proceedings.

Adriana turned and walked up the short flight of white marble stairs that joined the front lawn to the house. She walked through the entrance hall, stood at the bottom of the stairs, and called for Francesca.

"I'm coming, Mother," Francesca returned, and a moment later she descended the stairs.

"I see you've dressed early. That's wonderful. How is Valeria coming along?"

"She cannot decide which dress will enchant Mr. Kristiansen the most. I fear it will take her all day to decide and she'll miss the party entirely."

"Perhaps I should go to her. Please be a dear and ask Maria if they are ready to put out the tablecloths. If they are, will you see that they use the three six-foot-long matching cloths?" She lifted her skirts and began to ascend the stairs.

Adriana stood in the doorway of Valeria's room. "I'm certain whatever you decide to adorn yourself with will draw the admiration of Mr. Kristiansen."

Valeria looked anxiously at her mother. "Do you

really think so?"

"I know so." Adriana crossed the room and sat down at Valeria's gleaming polished-mahogany dressing table. She picked up the sterling silver brush, inspected it quickly, and said to no one in particular, "This vanity set needs to be polished."

"Mother, please help me decide," Valeria, in an uncharacteristic manner, implored.

"I've always thought when faced with indecision on such matters, it is best to wear whatever you're in the mood to wear."

"I'm in the mood to wear solid white, but that is impractical for croquet." Valeria drew her eyebrows together in a worried knot. "It would be wiser to wear this navy-blue skirt."

"Not if you are in the mood to wear white," Adriana said calmly. "If you are in a happy mood, then it is best not to cover that up with something that displeases you."

A huge smile spread across Valeria's face. "Thank you, Mother, so much." Valeria began to pull a white cotton dress over her head. "You know, I'm never this indecisive. I cannot for the life of me figure out why I'm acting like this."

"I would have no trouble helping you figure it out, if you would like my assistance."

"I know what you are going to say…"

"Well, then, I think we both know that you are besotted with Mr. Kristiansen. I will go even further to say he is equally besotted with you."

"My heart skips a beat to hear you say that," Valeria confided. "Will you help me fasten the back of this dress?"

"Come here and turn around." Adriana began the procedure. "There is everything right with the way you are feeling. You have your own heart and your own mind and it is capable of steering you in the right direction. I want you to know whichever direction you decide to take I will take with you. You have my love and my support, but do make certain that he is a kind and compassionate man fulfilled by his own pursuits. I would like to see you grow into your highest potential, and I think you will need a supportive man beside you to help along the way. It is a lifelong process, you know."

"I know you have done that, Mother, and I do see how Father adores you. I want to be just like you when I reach your age. Yes, I will be sure to monitor Mr. Kristiansen, but I have every confidence he is all of these things already."

"And so he may be." Adriana turned Valeria around and took a good look. "You look lovely. Are you ready to go down now?"

Within the hour, the carriages began to arrive, bringing well-dressed ladies and attentive gentlemen to the Siennas' front door. Sergio, the butler, directed the guests to the white-canvas marquee tent where the refreshments lay in wait.

Valeria and Francesca, both dressed in white, mingled amongst the guests, receiving many compliments on their appearance and exchanging social pleasantries. When Mrs. Davenworth's carriage arrived, Valeria looked around furtively and was disheartened to realize the dowager was alone. Francesca, following her gaze, shook her head slightly, giving the silent signal that Anders Kristiansen would arrive in good time.

Although he was the last guest to arrive, Anders Kristiansen stepped out of his carriage with the air of a man who was not in a hurry. Valeria watched from a distance as he exchanged what looked to be a joke with his driver; then proceed on to Sergio, giving him a slight nod in recognition before he turned and looked towards the gathered guests. With a casual gait, he walked towards the tent. Three times he was stopped en route and engaged by people who appeared to have previously made his acquaintance. One couple stood together and the lady extended her hand to Anders. As he took her hand, she motioned to an older woman to come forward. Valeria watched the introduction. Anders stood patiently and confidently and it was easy to tell, even from a distance, that the woman was impressed.

"He does indeed know how to charm the ladies, does he not?"

Valeria turned and looked into the eyes of Mrs. Davenworth. An unusually tall and genteel woman, perhaps a bit too thin, she carried herself with grace and poise. She was impeccably dressed in lavender skirts and lacy high-collar blouse, covered from head to toe in flounces of lacy ruffles. Over silver hair piled in a pompadour, she held a parasol which she twirled around at the handle in a distracted gesture that belied the fact that she was a focused woman who never missed a beat.

"Mrs. Davenworth, how lovely to see you. I'm so glad you could attend." Valeria reached out to take Cornelia Davenworth by her elegant hand. "To whom do you refer?"

"Why, the man you are gazing at so intently, of course." She smiled knowingly. "As you no doubt know,

I am his champion, and as you can imagine, I take an interest in how and where he spends his time. His mentor in Norway is my uncle, you know."

"Yes, I did know that. Mr. Kristiansen has said as much and he speaks of Mr. Jorgensen affectionately."

"And well Mr. Kristiansen should. My uncle raised the young man and saw to it that he developed his artistic talent. You should know of his reputation in Norway as a portrait artist. It is why I elected to invite him here to San Francisco. I thought he would do well. He is an orphan, of course, but to all of the Jorgensens, he is family."

"Mr. Kristiansen is an orphan? I had no idea." Valeria could not keep the surprise out of her voice. Now that she thought about it, Anders had never mentioned his family in any way.

"Well, now that he is in his mid-twenties—he is twenty-six to be exact—I consider that misfortune inconsequential. Mr. Kristiansen is a grown man and no longer tethered to such things as family."

Valeria, speechless, uttered the word that always saved her in such instances. "Indeed."

"Oh, quite right," Mrs. Davenworth continued. "Of course a lack of family can be a blessing *or* a curse. One never really knows where one fits in, but then there is also the freedom to create an unprotested future according to one's own desires."

"There is that." Valeria began to wonder if Mrs. Davenworth had some point in mind.

"I am sensitive to the probability that you cannot relate to such a background as Mr. Kristiansen's, nor he to yours. I imagine your father would be dismayed to learn the facts. He places such importance on family."

Valeria wondered how much Mrs. Davenworth knew and if her intent was to discourage further association between herself and Anders. "My father is a very compassionate man."

"And my uncle, Lars Jorgensen, is equally so. After all, the choice of family we are born into is in the hands of inviolable providence, but ultimately we are all left to make of life what we will." Mrs. Davenworth closed her parasol and guided Valeria beneath the tent. "As for me, I might never have left Norway had I not had the good fortune of meeting Mr. Davenworth. He was English, you know, and marrying him set my life onto a particular set of circumstances." She lowered her voice, leaned into Valeria, and spoke confidentially. "We women have to think very carefully about whom we align ourselves with. The stakes are very high as you must know."

Valeria gathered her meaning and immediately realized that Mrs. Davenworth was her ally.

"Never you mind about any of that, my sweet. When the time comes to consider Mr. Kristiansen seriously, I will be there vouching for his character. My uncle expects no less of me! I am often told I am the voice of reason, and as your father is known to be a reasonable man, I do not foresee any insurmountable obstacles before us." With a wink and a pinch of Valeria's cheek, Mrs. Davenworth swept self-assuredly out of the tent and opened her parasol, her skirts swishing behind her.

Valeria stepped to the buffet table and received a tall glass of iced lemonade. She felt Anders by her side and turned with a pleasant smile.

"I see my patroness has been bending your ear." He

winked at her. “Things looked conspiratorial so I thought I’d keep my distance.”

“No, not at all.”

“She speaks very highly of your family and surely you know Mrs. Davenworth is not one for gratuitous flattery,” Anders stated.

“No, she is not. We’ve known her for many years, well before she was widowed. Her husband was actually a business associate of my father.”

“Was he? I’m sorry I never had the pleasure of meeting him.”

“You would have liked him instantly. What a sense of humor he had,” Valeria reminisced, thinking of the short, stout Mr. Davenworth who wore a monocle and a pencil-thin mustache. He always carried wrapped taffy in his pocket for any child who crossed his path, and he remained perpetually jovial even in the most trying of circumstances.

An extremely wealthy and philanthropic man, Mr. Davenworth and his wife were communally loved and existed at the fulcrum of San Franciscan society. His absence, rather than detracting from his wife’s popularity, had elevated Mrs. Davenworth to the position of dowager grand dame of all that she surveyed.

“I do wonder sometimes if Mrs. Davenworth is ever sorry they did not have any children,” Valeria added.

“With many women, I would seriously question that, but Mrs. Davenworth has such a large circle of friends and so many activities to occupy her I think she gets along quite nicely. She has been an absolute God-send for me,” Anders admitted.

“It is no doubt her privilege.”

"Were it not for the generosity of Mrs. Davenworth and her uncle, I may never have come to San Francisco, and I may never have had the life-enhancing honor of meeting the most captivating young lady in town."

Valeria, unaccustomed to such direct flattery, changed the subject. "Have you spoken to my father yet?"

"I have not, but I see him there with a croquet mallet in his hand." Anders gestured towards the front lawn.

"I wouldn't want to keep you from mingling with the guests, but if you would like to say hello to my father then I'll go with you," Valeria offered.

"Oh, mingling with you is more than enough to keep me happy, but let's go anyway." He offered her his arm and they walked down the slope to the front of the lawn together, her hand upon his supportive left arm.

As they approached, her father straightened up from his shot. "Valeria, watch closely if you want to see how the game is won," he boasted.

"He is merely experiencing a temporary stroke of luck," his opponent quipped, striking a conscious pose with his right hand balancing his lean stature against the tip of his mallet. At the knee, his right leg crossed over his left as if he was preparing to be photographed.

"Valeria, you remember Giancarlo Vargas who manages the Genoa Hotel downtown, don't you?" Domenico swept a presenting hand towards the perfectly coiffed young man.

"Of course I do. How nice to see you again, Mr. Vargas."

The young man lowered to an ostentatious bow. "You and your sister grow more beautiful each time I see you."

Valeria wondered where Francesca was, now that Giancarlo Vargas was present. She wanted to deflect his attention off of herself and onto Francesca. She looked around, but there was no sign of her sister. If Valeria knew her father, Giancarlo had been invited for the sole purpose of securing his friendship with their family. He was exactly the sort of man her father wanted to see one of his daughters marry. The man had a stable occupation and an Italian lineage.

That meant little to Valeria and she considered Giancarlo little more than a sycophant: too eager, too flashy, and too impressed with himself. Because he had been born in Florence, Italy, he spoke Italian as his first language, making his English too formal and too exaggerated. Twice, Valeria had met Giancarlo Vargas in the lobby of the Genoa Hotel—once with her mother and the other time with Francesca. Both times, Valeria found Mr. Vargas's manner intrusive and presumptuous.

"Mr. Vargas, I'd like to introduce you to Mr. Anders Kristiansen," Valeria deferred. "He is new to San Francisco and comes to us from Norway."

"You're a long way from home, Mr. Kristiansen. Please, tell me what it is that brings you to San Francisco."

"You could say I am a man who is following his destiny, Mr. Vargas," Anders said plainly.

"Mr. Kristiansen is an artist," her father interjected.

"An artist!" Mr. Vargas said with a note of surprise as if he were trying to imagine such an occupation. Valeria did not like what his tone implied.

"A very gifted artist," she included as she glanced

from Mr. Vargas to her father. Both men were looking at Anders, trying to size him up.

"So art is your destiny? Do tell." Mr. Vargas's tone dripped with condescension.

"Art is what is leading me to my destiny. It is merely a vehicle," Anders replied steadily.

"Oh, what luxury to have the latitude of time to follow the stars." Mr. Vargas sighed dismissively. "I'm a practical man myself. I believe in taking things into my own hands and molding them to my benefit."

Anders laughed, defusing the tension. He ran a hand through his hair and smiled. "It is an unusual enough trade, I'll give you that, Mr. Vargas, but somebody has to do it."

Valeria glowed with pride. The ease of Anders' quick banter confirmed her belief that she stood beside an exceptional man whose relaxed manner and steady gaze would not rise to the blatant provocation of Giancarlo Vargas. She recognized Anders would not be intimidated by any man, and without thought she placed her hand back on his arm.

"Father, if you'll excuse us, I want to go and find Francesca." Valeria looked over her shoulder, scanning the yard for her sister.

"But Mr. Kristiansen has not had the opportunity to try his hand at croquet," Domenico observed. "I was looking forward to the challenge. Now is the opportune time, if Mr. Vargas has had enough of my obviously superior command of the game."

"I can see when I have been beaten, and have the humility to bow out gracefully, Mr. Sienna." Vargas returned his mallet to the rack stand. He took an encroaching step towards Valeria.

"Good, then that settles it. Mr. Kristiansen, will you indulge me?"

"I wouldn't want to put you to shame, Mr. Sienna. I can see you have been enjoying a winning streak, and although I hate to disrupt it, it is not my way to shy away from a challenge," Anders chided.

"Nothing doing." Her father handed him a mallet. Valeria waved her hand and walked quickly back up the slope towards the marquee so that the newly released Mr. Vargas wouldn't follow her.

Anders beat Domenico Sienna twice in two rounds of the game. When Domenico conceded defeat, he lifted his hat from the mallet rack, signifying he'd had enough. Domenico placed a hand on Anders' shoulder, steering him off course.

"I believe it is you that presents me with a challenge," Domenico began.

"By any chance, would that be a veiled reference, Mr. Sienna?" Anders walked beside him with an easy stride.

"It might be. It depends entirely upon your position." Domenico stopped and looked up, holding Anders in a deliberate eye-lock.

"The air is full of your unspoken words, sir. I suspect there is a question lingering somewhere."

"How astute of you, Mr. Kristiansen, yes, there is. I have noticed you have amassed a fan club of the women in my life. You show little attempt at withdrawing your attention from my youngest daughter, and the question would be somewhere along the lines of your intentions."

"Well then, I will oblige you with my response. I am

besotted with Valeria and intend on showering her with attention for as long as she will permit."

"As I suspected." Domenico stopped, removed his hat, and placed his free hand into his coat pocket.

Although he was noticeably shorter than Anders, he held his gaze forcibly. The sun shone down on his hair, creating a shimmer like polished black obsidian. His eyes narrowed and his voice lowered with the resonance of authority.

"I don't have to tell you that my girls hold my heart. I have two grown sons whom I do not have to look after as closely. They are away in Italy finishing their education and they are not a worry to me. With girls, it is always different. One feels the need to protect them always. When the time does come for them to marry, I want to be sure it is a compatible match, for a part of me thereafter will be sharing the responsibility of their protection with another man. I want to see them both cherished and financially secure. I want to see them both continue to pursue their interests, because I have seen the fulfillment that comes from doing so in their mother's life. Francesca is sure of herself, and mature beyond her years, but Valeria is more impressionable. She has yet to grow into her own confidence."

"That may only be from a lack of opportunity. All things that fly have to go through the process of testing their wings. I cannot help but tell you I detect strength and self-assurance in Valeria's character. I know she is capable of rising to any occasion."

"No doubt you are correct. She is so much like her mother in that respect. I want to point out Valeria has a big heart and extends her trust easily. She assumes the world is a safe place and oftentimes charges into things without looking before her. Her mother tells me Valeria is smitten with you, and I can see that for myself. Whatever the future may hold, it is now that concerns me. I want to be certain you have a firm grasp on the repercussions of your continued attention towards my daughter."

"In other words, you want to know if I am sincere. I assure you, Mr. Sienna, I am very sincere and I do not take this matter lightly."

"Very good then, we understand each other, do we not?"

"We do, sir, thoroughly," Anders confirmed.

Chapter Ten

March 18, 1999
West Hollywood, California

"What's this all about?" Lucia pulled out a chair across from her sister. They sat outside on the sidewalk in front of the King's Head Café in West Hollywood amidst the hum of traffic and the flow of patrons looking for available seating on Beverly Boulevard. "You sounded funny on the phone."

"I sounded funny?"

"You sounded mysterious," Lucia clarified.

"I didn't want to get into it on the phone. I thought I'd wait to talk to you in person."

"All right, I'm listening." Lucia settled back into her chair and looked at Anna expectantly.

"You're not going to believe this, but Kevin brought up the subject of marriage the other day."

"Why wouldn't I believe that? It's perfectly understandable to me. Isn't it to you?" Lucia laughed. "What did you say when he brought up the subject?"

"I skirted the issue, of course." Anna's tone suggested Lucia should know that.

"Wait a minute, did he just bring up the subject or did he ask you to marry him?"

"Well, it seemed to me he was testing the waters, but what he said was 'God help me, I'm married to a witch.' I'm not sure I was supposed to hear it, but that's exactly what he said," Anna told her.

"Wait a minute, back up, I'm getting lost. Were you doing something that made him call you a witch, or was he just making a general observation because he's had enough time to realize that you are a little touched in that way?"

"In *what* way?" Anna sounded defensive.

"Come on, Anna, anyone who knows you knows you're bent towards the uncanny, and I mean that with nothing but love." Lucia tried to suppress a smile. "You're the same way that Mom was—obviously these things run in families."

Anna felt the immediate tug of her heartstrings at the mention of their mother, who had died of leukemia two and a half years earlier. Her illness had been a harrowing experience to both her and Lucia, absolutely draining them emotionally for the two years prior to her death. Her slow decline compounded the loss of their father when they were only teenagers, and now that both parents were gone, Anna and Lucia only had each other. Anna conjured the memory of their mother's face, her tall elegance, and demure ways, and recalled that she, too, had an intuitive ability that everyone who knew her remarked upon.

"I don't know that I'm anywhere near the way Mom was." Anna leaned back. "Do you remember how she always knew what we were up to when we were little? There was no point in ever trying to fool her about anything because she always knew the truth."

"Of course, because you've always been a terrible liar. Everything you're thinking is always written on your face. You were the one who always gave us away to Mom, not me," Lucia reminded.

"That's not entirely true," Anna volleyed. "I remember the time you tried to sneak out the upstairs window at night and found Mom sitting on the garden bench under the tree you used because she'd picked up on what you were thinking practically before you even decided to do it. She could tell just by looking at you!"

"You're right about that." Lucia nodded. "Mom was something else altogether, wasn't she? I'm convinced she was clairvoyant. I think she knew how to read us both. I really do miss her every day. I think of her every time I see a sunset, every time I feel the change of seasons in the air, every time I see the full moon. She made such an event out of the little things in life, didn't she?"

"She definitely did. She placed great importance on ceremonies and symbolism and things like that," Anna said. "I see so many things the same way she did because she taught us how."

"I do, too. What she did to the exact spot where Dad had his car wreck is a perfect example."

"Well, a lot of people do a similar thing. I see markers on the side of the road all the time. Standing crosses with bouquets of flowers under them at the scene of a fatal accident. It's a commemoration of a particular place where something significant happened."

"Yes, but it was so much more to Mom than that," Lucia reminded Anna. "That's why she buried the key where Dad got in the accident. Do you recall that night? It was only two days after Dad died, but somehow Mom managed to set aside her grief in order to take care of business. She woke us up after midnight and told us to get in the car because we were going to conduct a ceremony."

"I remember." Anna cast her eyes down, then looked back up at Lucia. "She was always teaching us, no matter the circumstances."

"She was. Mom taught us everything she believed. She was unselfish in that way."

"I remember the cross she hammered into the ground and how she knelt and buried the key beside it, then camouflaged it with a rock. It was so important to Mom that we understand. I remember kneeling beside her to pray, and how she looked at me and asked if I understood the meaning of the word *portal*."

Lucia's eyes twinkled. "I remember you didn't have a clue."

"How was I supposed to know Mom wanted to leave Dad the key to a door so he could come back whenever he wanted?"

"Well, I can't say I had a better understanding at the time. I knew a *portal* was an entrance, or a door of some kind, but I didn't know until that night that a *portal* was spontaneously created at the scene of an accident."

"Mom made it sound as if Dad chose that specific spot to walk through to the other side. She told me time was trapped, or rather stopped permanently, so that Dad could come and go through the door between worlds. She meant it and had absolutely no doubt." Anna folded her arms across her chest as if a chill had reached her.

"Not to change the subject," Anna continued, "but you do know some people can look through these doors if they're sensitive to such things, right?"

Lucia narrowed her eyes. "I do know, and I think that's the entire point. It's about sensitivity, isn't it? Maybe places where tragic events take place are more energetically charged, so to speak."

"Probably so, but once again, you have to be sensitive to it. Mom was definitely sensitive. You're kind of that way too, Lucia."

"I'm sensitive to a certain degree, but not as much as you are. I'll admit I have a certain amount of sensitivity with episodes of telepathy and that kind of thing, but when I do, it's always with you. I don't go around operating that way with everybody, you know. I assume it's common enough in families, more so with siblings who are as close as we are, but I pretty much stop right there. You, on the other hand, are what I consider hyper-sensitive to everything and—

"I know, I know," Anna interrupted. "That's why I'm studying the subject. I've been told that if you learn how to develop your intuitive abilities, they become more pronounced. People who start to develop themselves intuitively are typically warned to be careful, though. It's said once they do, strange things start to happen because they're more sensitive. I'm not going to worry about that. My thinking is I have a responsibility to develop myself. It's like a moral obligation, know what I mean?"

"I totally understand. You're just saying that as long as you have it, you should learn how to use it, right?" Lucia clarified.

"That's right."

"I get it. Let's get back to the bigger subject. What were you doing when Kevin mentioned marriage?"

"I was reading his auric field. I just wanted to see what was there, and I needed the practice. You have to keep in practice, you know."

"Okay, that may have set off the subject of being a witch, which I'm sure he didn't mean literally, but what about the marriage part?"

Anna replayed the conversation in her mind for the hundredth time. "Well, when I told him I wasn't a witch, I followed it by pointing out that we aren't married, and then he said we should be."

"So, is there something wrong with him saying that?"

"Kind of." Anna looked away, avoiding the subject.

"Anna, you obviously have something to say so let's hear it," Lucia encouraged.

A waiter appeared and placed two glasses of water and two menus on the table, then discreetly disappeared. Anna took her time looking over the menu, quietly closed it, and slid it to her right.

"I've been having funny dreams lately."

"Dreams about what?"

"Well, they're confusing, but it's as if I keep having the exact same dream over and over. In it, I'm running and shouting frantically for Kevin, but then again, I'm not even sure the person I'm looking for is Kevin. I mean, it feels as if it's Kevin, but in a way it's somebody else."

Lucia leaned forward. "Are you running towards something or away from something?"

"Away from something, but then again I'm also looking for Kevin. I'm fairly certain it's Kevin. All I know is I'm terrified. Also, I'm aware of water in the dream, large turbulent waves. I'm thinking that whenever someone dreams of water, it usually refers to one's emotional level." Anna explained as well as she could. "This dream seems to indicate horrific emotional turmoil."

"Well, I'm not sure you can generalize about water's meaning in a dream, although I know there are plenty of books out there on dream interpretation which suggest you can. Take me, for instance. I've always been afraid of water, so if it were my dream, it might symbolize something I am really afraid of. Dreams tend to be in a language specific to the dreamer. Can you figure out what the emotional turmoil concerns?"

"That's just it. I don't know. All I know is it doesn't feel good and it scares me. I'm either subconsciously interpreting my current relationship with Kevin and not liking what I find, or my dreams are precognitive and something ahead of us is really going to be bad." Anna let out an audible breath.

When most people talk about their dreams, they are merely recounting the nighttime musings of their mind as it dwells upon the past day's events. With Anna, it was different and had been since she was a small child. Sometimes Anna's dreams were prophetic. She had dreamed of earthquakes before they happened and of people in her life before she met them.

"Anna..." Lucia lowered her head and spoke softly as the waiter reappeared. "I don't know what to tell you, but I think I understand why you're hesitant to talk about marriage with Kevin. I don't know what your dreams mean, but I do know that love outweighs everything, even fear."

When the waiter had retreated with their order, Anna finally said what was on her mind. "I agree, love outweighs everything, but I have this feeling of inevitable doom, as if it's hovering above me or lying in wait for me to put certain wheels in motion. It's as if something is going to happen, or something has already happened but I can't remember it. Honestly, I feel like I am fated to be with Kevin forever, but I'm wary of the future. I can't quite put it into words. I'm afraid, that's all."

"I don't think you should let fear of the unknown stand in the way of love. I know you and Kevin truly love each other. You say you feel fated to be with him and that tells me a lot. I think all any of us can do is take things step-by-step as each step presents itself. What you have to ask yourself is if marriage is the next appropriate step. Now that the subject of marriage has been broached, Kevin will no doubt bring it up again, so you'd be well advised to have a ready answer. Just think about what you want out of the relationship. Think about where you see yourself this time next year."

Anna admired Lucia's ability to give mature, sound advice. She could always count on it and more often than not she agreed completely with her sister. Where Anna clouded reason with emotions, Lucia always saw through the clouds, and Anna reminded herself once again that she was astoundingly lucky to have Lucia as a confidant.

If she thought about it, Anna could not imagine herself ever without Kevin. They were used to each other, compatible together, interested in each other, mutually supportive, and most definitely in love. When they were together it was thrilling, and when they were not they were forever on each other's minds. For all of her idiosyncrasies, she felt accepted and understood by Kevin, and because of that a part of her retained a quiet fascination that love and luck had brought her to the arms of such a stabilizing man.

He was good for her, grounded her, and gave her constant love and attention. Kevin possessed the rare quality of unselfconscious confidence in himself. It gave him an authoritative air that made it all the more intriguing that he was also a kind and compassionate man.

Anna knew that if she had the power to manufacture the perfect man for her, he would end up being exactly like Kevin Townsend. Her fears were based on so little, she rationalized. She shouldn't be responding this way to the prospect of marriage. They were, after all, only dreams, but the thing that unnerved her was the fact she couldn't put her finger on exactly what her recurring dreams meant. She assumed they must be important or they wouldn't recur so frequently.

What worried her was the knowledge that sometimes her dreams came true and sometimes they didn't. She had no way of knowing which dreams were prophetic and which were not, so her recent dreams of Kevin were perplexing and their uncertainty made her nervous.

Lucia was right, Anna decided as she drove back to her apartment. *I should let time develop things and take things step-by-step with no fear. What exists between Kevin and me is true love, and I would be a fool not to allow it to take its course.*

Chapter Eleven

August 24, 1902
San Francisco

Domenico Sienna seemed to be softening. It had been more than three months since his conversation with Anders Kristiansen at the family's garden party and he was convinced of Anders' sincerity towards Valeria. Surprisingly, he found himself embracing the thought of having an artist as a son-in-law.

He shook his head as he lit a cigar and thought of how much he had changed since coming to America. He once thought a reliable, independent trade was the only sensible way to ensure monetary security. Now he took financial risks into uncharted business arenas that required him to relinquish full control and delegate responsibility to people outside of his extended family.

That was only the start of the changes he considered as he placed his cigar in the lead-crystal ashtray and settled into his favorite chair with a tumbler of scotch beside him. His world had expanded, it seemed. There were different people in it now—friends and associates from other walks of life he never would have met had he stayed in his native Italy. These people enriched his life and brought a wider spectrum of thought and information to him. He had parlayed their influence into better business dealings than he could have ever manufactured on his own.

America, he thought, was indeed the great melting

pot it was reputed to be and everybody appeared to benefit.

He turned his thoughts back to Valeria and Anders. It would be any week now that Anders would ask for her hand in marriage, of this Domenico had no doubt. He could see the signs from everyone around him, although they all took great measures to mask their encouragement.

Domenico let his mind muse upon the ways of women. It was amusing to him that they approached the business of Valeria's romance with a studied indirectness aimed only at making the courtship appear as if it were his own idea. They tiptoed around him, pointing out the many selling points of Anders Kristiansen: the contacts and connections he had made in San Francisco in such a short amount of time; his impressive list of patrons; his steady work schedule; his social popularity; and the enormous flattery of his attentions upon Valeria out of all the eligible young ladies in town.

They need not have wasted their time. Domenico could see the facts for himself, but he did love the sport of watching the women in his life twitter on as they sought his permission on the subject. *I'm a changed man,* he thought to himself. *Anders Kristiansen is not even an Italian.*

He supposed the changes in him had come about at the hands of his wife, Adriana. She was beautiful and sophisticated and people naturally gravitated to her. Her favorite pastime was entertaining, and the invitations she extended were always reciprocated. As the years of their marriage progressed, Domenico had unwittingly grown from an austere, serious-minded young man to a man who actually enjoyed the pleasures and frivolity of society. Adriana made it all so easy, and her way of doting on him as she did so gave him a higher plateau of social confidence and self-esteem. As their circle of acquaintances expanded, Domenico found he had cultivated a more tolerant attitude accompanied by a more lenient mind towards everyone. He decided this was good for business as well as pleasure.

Lost in his reverie, he did not see Valeria enter the room.

"Pardon me, Father," she said. "I wanted to bring you today's mail. I'm not disturbing you, am I?"

"No, not at all. Let me see what you have there." He took the small stack of envelopes from her extended hand. He sifted through them, and as he suspected from her uncharacteristic interest in the mail, he withdrew an envelope with the initials of Anders Kristiansen embossed on the back.

He looked up at Valeria, who stood expectantly nearby, and gestured for her to take a seat across from him. With great flourish and histrionics, he opened the envelope. Wordlessly, he scanned its contents, replaced the letter in the envelope, and set it on the table beside him. Then he picked up the newspaper and began to unfold the pages.

"Father, how could you!" Valeria burst forth.

"I'm only trying your self-restraint," he teased, but Valeria rose from her seat and made as if she would snatch the letter up for herself. "Sit down, sit down." He chuckled. "I'll tell you plainly that your young man has requested an audience with me, and I do not believe he means to include anyone else."

"When?" Valeria demanded.

"Three days from now, which will be Saturday and suits me perfectly. The young man must have studied my habits," Domenico observed.

"But Father, you know that Francesca and I will be taking our painting lesson on Saturday! We won't be here," she said impatiently.

Domenico suppressed a smile. "Let me remind you of what I said only a moment ago. I don't believe he intends to include anyone else." Valeria started to rise to her feet but he held up a halting hand. "And these, my dear one, might possibly be the longest three days of your life."

* * *

Anders Kristiansen was neither a nervous nor a self-conscious man, but he had had a devil of a time dressing for his audience with Domenico Sienna. Nothing he tried on seemed to fit the seriousness of the occasion, and finally he sat down at his desk and looked around his bedroom. The entire contents of his closet lay strewn about every available surface in the room. He took a deep breath and decided to start anew.

First, he selected an appropriate hat, then he riffled through the pile on his bed and found a conservative waistcoat. From there, he found a matching coat that he partnered with complimentary trousers, which he then fastened with secure suspenders. "Shoes," he muttered aloud, "black, no embellishment—a man is judged by the appearance of his shoes." He selected a pair and polished them more in an act of dispersing energy than out of necessity.

Once assembled, he stood before the dresser mirror

and turned in all directions, surveying the effect. He reached for the chain of his watch and took it out of his breast pocket as if doing so would make time move faster. He paced the room then decided to replace the jumble of clothes into his closet. He moved as if by rote—running answers to imagined questions through his mind for the millionth time. *Carmel,* he thought. *I wonder what Mr. Sienna will think of that.*

His carriage driver arrived early, so Anders offered him a glass of water, reminding himself he must be perfectly on time. Arriving early would seem too anxious, and being late, of course, irreverent. He checked his watch again and strode back inside. "I'll leave in ten minutes," he said to himself, and that is exactly what he did.

* * *

Sergio ushered Anders into the house with the dignity and jurisdiction befitting his post. Anders was grateful for the lack of small talk, for he had specific business on his mind which he had rehearsed and he did not want to see it sidetracked. He walked into the drawing room expecting to see Domenico Sienna seated in the wing-backed chair, but he was not.

The big doors to the patio were open, and after standing a moment in the room, Anders walked outside. He looked to the right, then to the left, but could see no sign of the man. Hesitatingly, he followed the red-brick walk to the garden on the south side of the house where Domenico Sienna stood before the marble fountain with both hands in his pockets.

He was hatless and without a coat, and Anders had the impression Mr. Sienna was unconcerned with whether or not the undulating fountain would spray him. He seemed not to hear Anders as he approached, yet he turned instinctively the second he was behind him.

"There you are, young man. Please, take off your coat. It's a lovely day with no women around to impress. Let's enjoy the afternoon, shall we?"

Anders laid his coat on the gray granite garden bench and placed his hat upon it as well. He ran a hand through his hair and came closer to the fountain.

"I commissioned this piece myself." Domenico waved a hand toward the fountain. "It's made only of Italian marble."

"Yes, Valeria told me as much the first time I came to this house. It is majestic."

"The first time you came to this house? Let me see if I can recall. When was that, Mr. Kristiansen?"

"A little less than four months ago, sir."

"Yes, of course, that's right. Seems longer than that, doesn't it? Funny how time passes."

Anders nodded distractedly. Things were not going as he had envisioned. He had expected to have a formal audience with Mr. Sienna in the drawing room of his house, and their visit would be conducted somewhere along the lines of a business meeting wherein Anders would simply state why he had come and wait for Mr. Sienna's reaction.

He had prepared himself with an arsenal of answers to questions of his own worthiness—financially and otherwise. Now that things had gotten off to such an unpredictable start, Anders was uncertain of how to proceed.

"Let me make this easy on you, Mr. Kristiansen. You

have come to talk something over with me this afternoon. I am all too willing to hear what it is," Domenico began.

Anders followed his lead. "That's right, sir. I have come to talk to you about your daughter, Valeria."

"Ah, one of my favorite subjects and as I suspected." Domenico crossed to the empty garden bench across from the one that held Anders' coat and hat and gestured for Anders to find a seat for himself.

Anders seated himself beside his belongings and steadied his gaze upon Domenico. "It has been four months now since I made her acquaintance, and since then I have thought of little else other than how to be worthy of her. I am satisfied now that I have secured a position financially that holds great promise for the future, and I could never imagine another who would adore your daughter more. As I ponder my future, I realize she is my primary goal and ambition and that everything else I do weighs upon whether or not it would contribute to Valeria's happiness. You see, I do not see myself at all in the future without her by my side. Therefore, sir, I have come to ask you most respectfully for Valeria's hand in marriage."

Domenico clasped his hands together, momentarily suggesting the perfunctory applause after a performance. "Well then, there it is." He rose, walked to the bubbling fountain, and turned around to Anders. "I can only say now it is time to discuss your plans and prospects in detail. You say you feel confident about your future finances. Tell me more."

Anders pivoted in his seat to face him. "I draw a magnificent wage for the portraits I paint and have been doing so since I arrived in San Francisco. At five hundred dollars per portrait, I have already completed fifteen and have a waiting list of a dozen more. All of this has been achieved with very little word other than that of Mrs. Davenworth, which leads me to conclude that with a modest amount of advertising, I could far exceed that which I have already accomplished. There are other communities to the north, south, and east of San Francisco which remain unexplored, and I have not heard of any competition that would hinder me," Anders said.

"Have you any investments?" Domenico prodded.

"I do not at the moment, sir. I see the wisdom in investments but feel the need to retain an expert on such."

"Where do you intend to live? Certainly not in Mrs. Davenworth's guest house!"

"The answer to that ties in nicely with my career. You see, along with developing my reputation as a portrait artist, I have begun to paint landscapes as well. They are something very popular in Europe and in Norway—one rarely sees anything else. I am confident that the popularity of landscapes will sweep America, and I believe developing both subject matters will diversify my talents.

"I arrived at this conclusion when I first came to America. I spent some time in a growing community just south of here called Carmel. It is on the Monterey Peninsula and is breathtakingly beautiful. It is new in development, and land there sells at a fair price. I have my eye on a small parcel of land near the sea and have met the man who owns it as well. Do you know anything about the area?" Anders asked hopefully.

"What I know about it is exactly what you've just told me, and also that the area is attracting all types of artisans. What I don't like about it is that it is not in San Francisco. Are you proposing to marry Valeria and move her away from her home and family?" Domenico spoke in a voice thick with disapproval.

Anders was prepared for Domenico's response. "I understand your concern and am sympathetic, but Carmel is less than a four and a half hour train ride from San Francisco and is in an atmosphere that would be a welcome change of pace for all of your family. Each time your family visits, it will be like taking a vacation, for Carmel is steadily becoming a splendid seaside resort. Valeria's relocation to Carmel would be nothing as drastic as the move you and Mrs. Sienna made from your native land of Italy. In the grand scheme of things, we would be all but neighbors."

"But tell me, why Carmel? Why not stay in San Francisco?" Domenico asked.

"The beauty of the peninsula is absolutely inspirational, which is essential to all painters. Already, an artists' community has taken root, and the business prospects are attractive. Alongside this is the lure of joining a community on the ground level and watching it grow. It is tempting to become involved in an official community capacity because, of course, one hopes to help build an ideal environment for one's children."

Valeria's father remained disturbingly silent for an uncomfortable amount of time—then extended his hand to Anders.

"I will give this my deepest consideration, and will send for you Monday afternoon if you will indulge me a little time."

"As it should be, sir," Anders replied.

Chapter Twelve

March 25, 1999
Los Angeles

At seven o'clock, Kevin shut down his computer and left Williams and Khan for the day. He stood at the elevator with his briefcase in hand and waited for the lift to reach the thirty-third floor. He took a deep breath and ran his hand through his hair as if the gesture would sweep away the day's concerns and prepare him for the evening ahead. As the elevator's ascending numbers lit up, he began to pace and clutched his briefcase a little tighter, for in it was the ring he intended to give Anna.

The ring was an estate piece—a two carat emerald-cut diamond, set in platinum that he had painstakingly selected from Nobel Jewelers in Santa Monica earlier that day. He had looked at rings in Tiffany's and Harry Winston, until he came to the realization that nothing contemporary would ever suit Anna.

Her taste in all things, from literature to decorative arts, leaned toward the antiquated, and she had a propensity for relics from the past.

She might be completely surprised at the ring, Kevin thought, but she would not be disappointed.

When the elevator finally arrived, he rode it down to the parking garage where he unlocked his Jeep. Taking out his cell phone, he dialed their apartment where he knew Anna waited.

He had not intended to leave the office this late, but

he had received a phone call from his mother in Massachusetts, and once they started talking about his plans, the conversation became lengthy. His mother was extremely pleased and told him she had wondered when he would propose. She considered her son to be a thoroughly stable, responsible young man and it was only fitting that he settled into the domesticity of married life.

She loved Anna and identified with her offbeat ways, for she saw a bit of herself in her future daughter-in-law. Both women possessed an artistic temperament and both managed to lead an unconventional life. She liked the fact that Anna painted, and felt her influence would encourage Kevin to do the same. Her only concern when it came to her son was that he would neglect his artistic talent in exchange for his law practice, and she did not want to see his talent go to waste.

She continuously reminded Kevin to keep balance in his life or he would become too serious a man. "Anna is perfect for you," she gushed. "Call me as soon as she accepts!"

Kevin decided to surprise Anna with the ring at home. He knew that if he took her to a fancy restaurant in town she would grow suspicious. He had brought up the subject of marriage, quite by accident, only once and it occurred to him that in the nine months of knowing Anna, they had never seriously discussed the prospect. It seemed to him Anna had blanched when he broached the subject, but perhaps that was only his imagination.

Their lives were entwined to the point where they acted as if they were already married. *This is evidential reasoning,* he thought to himself. *Of course she'll want to get married.* He smiled as he realized he was thinking like a lawyer. Within seconds, a wave of doubt surged through his mind. Anna, he considered, was perhaps the most unpredictable person he had ever known, and it would be anybody's guess how she would respond to the presentation of an engagement ring.

He hit the send button on his cell phone and waited for the connection.

"Hello, beautiful," he greeted when Anna picked up the phone.

"Are you on your way home?"

"I'm just pulling out of the garage. I'll be home in about fifteen minutes, traffic allowing. What are you doing?"

"Oh, not much of anything. How was your day? Anything new?"

"I'll save it until I get home, all right?"

"Okay. I'll see you in a little bit. Drive safely."

"I will." He placed the phone back in its charger as every nerve in his body tightened. He tried to envision Anna's response to the ring he carried and was unsettled by his own nervousness. Maybe he should have tested the subject of marriage one more time, then he might have a better feel of her attitude towards the prospect. Maybe then he wouldn't be catching her completely off-guard.

As if watching his own thoughts sail through his head, he reminded himself he had already made the decision to give her the ring, and tonight he would follow through. He may be springing this on her out of the blue, but by the night's end, he would have his answer.

Kevin paused outside the apartment door and squared his shoulders. He put his key in the lock and started to turn it, but the door swung open and he could hear music coming from inside.

He entered the living room where the aroma of unidentified herbs enticed his senses. He walked towards the dining room and found the dining table draped in fine Irish linen with a silver candelabra on each end. The lit candles cast a shimmering glow on the silver ice bucket that held a bottle of unopened champagne. Waterford crystal sparkled, and sterling silver place settings, inherited from Anna's grandmother, rested upon the cloth. Just as Kevin thought tonight must be some special occasion he must have forgotten, Anna appeared wearing a floor-length white linen dress, and he remembered it was indeed a special occasion for his own reasons.

Anna looked lovely. Her long dark hair lay in splendid contrast to the dress she wore, and upon closer inspection, Kevin noticed she wore no jewelry save for the diamond stud earrings he had given her on their six-month anniversary. His gaze traveled to her feet, on which she had light pink ballet slippers. For some reason unknown to him, Anna had gone to great measures to look her best and the effort paid off spectacularly.

"It sure is a pleasure to come home and find all this."

"You're worth it."

"It must have taken you hours to put all of this together. Is there any reason I should know about? By the way, you look beautiful."

"Nothing is too much for the man I love, and thank you." Anna walked over and gave him a hug.

"I haven't missed a special occasion, have I?"

"Not necessarily. Anyway, we create our own special occasions as we go along, don't we?" she asked.

"You could say that, but seriously, Anna, why tonight? It's not even a weekend." Kevin wanted to know. For the life of him, he couldn't arrive at any reason Anna should act as if this night was a special occasion.

"I was only thinking you might want to talk to me, and I wanted to provide a fitting background. That's all."

"Oh, I get it, it's like that, is it?" Kevin was starting to get the picture.

"Yes, it's like that. I know what I'm talking about, what are you talking about?"

Kevin drew in his breath and thought to himself, *She's not doing this again, is she?*

"What are you thinking about?" Anna stood casually with a mischievous look on her face.

"Well, right now I'm thinking about that bottle of champagne, and I'm wondering if you're reading my thoughts again"

"Can I pour you a glass?" She reached over and removed the bottle from the ice bucket. Deftly, she uncorked the bottle without spilling a drop and ceremoniously poured two glasses. She handed one to Kevin and lifted hers to touch his.

"Let's sit down." Kevin turned and led the way into the living room.

"I thought you'd never ask." Anna laughed, following behind him until they sat side-by-side on the living room sofa. "Shall we call this meeting to order?"

"Anna, cut it out." Kevin took a swallow of his champagne and set the glass down slowly.

"Well, you have something to ask me, don't you?" Anna sat perfectly still, facing Kevin with a look on her face that unnerved him.

"You're taking all the fun out of this for me," he protested.

"I apologize for that, but just so you know, I'm having enough fun for both of us."

"I can see that." He began to execute his plan. He stood up quickly and walked to where his briefcase lay by the front door. He reached for the handle and hesitated. "Maybe you should close your eyes for a second."

"I'll follow your command." She covered her eyes with both hands.

Kevin sat down beside her and placed the briefcase on the coffee table. The click of metal sounded as he released the locks, and he reached inside and picked up a red leather box. He cleared his throat and got down on bended knee.

"You can open your eyes now," he began. "I've been thinking of this moment for practically a month. I've been searching my mind for the right words to say, but I know the words will come if I speak from my heart. These past nine months have been the best of my life, simply because you've been in them. You are my strength and you are my weakness. You are everything a man could aspire to, and I can't imagine my life without you by my side. I feel the sanctity in our love, and I want to create something sacred and permanent between us. I want to marry you, Anna Lucera. I want to create a life with you that brings us both love and joy. Nothing in the world would make me prouder than to call you my wife.

In short, will you marry me?"

"Yes, my love, I will marry you," she whispered.

Kevin opened the box, took her left hand in his, and slipped the ring on her finger. She looked down at the ring and a look of amazement spread across her face. She held her hand out before her and a look of pure love appeared in her eyes.

"If this is the beginning of marriage, I like being married to you already."

"Do you like it?" Kevin asked anxiously.

"I love it! Where in the world did you find this ring? It's the most gorgeous thing I've ever seen." She turned her hand this way and that, viewing the diamond from all angles.

"Well, I did look around a bit, but I ultimately decided only an estate piece would suit you. I ended up going to Nobel Jewelers in Santa Monica. I was told this ring came from an estate up north and is close to a hundred years old."

"I absolutely love it. Never in my wildest dreams would I have imagined such a beautiful ring. Thank you, Kevin. I'll love it forever!"

"But you did know I was going to give you a ring, didn't you?"

"Why in the world would you ask me that?" She reached for her glass as if the gesture would re-route the question.

"Because I want to know if you knew I planned to give you a ring," he pressed.

"Yes. I mean…I thought of course someday you would."

"What I'm asking you is if you knew I was going to

give you a ring *tonight,*" he said pointedly.

"Specifically tonight?"

"Yes, Anna, specifically tonight." He tried to hold her gaze.

She took a long sip from her glass.

"Anna?"

"Yes?"

"Answer the question, please." A patience that belied the need for urgency crept into his voice. "I want to know if you knew I would ask you to marry me tonight," Kevin repeated the question.

"I can't say I *knew,* but I had a funny feeling."

"So a funny feeling is all it takes for you to set up tonight as if it were Christmas? Surely it's more than that!"

"Well, all I can say is it seemed like the right thing to do, just in case you were going to ask me to marry you."

Kevin decided to let the matter go because the need to immediately gather this attractive, mysterious woman in his arms overrode his curiosity completely.

Perhaps he would never understand the makings of the woman he loved. Perhaps it was enough to recognize she had intuitive insights that were reliable more often than not. If he pressed her to explain how she knew the things she knew, she would grow evasive, and he wondered if the reason was because she didn't think he'd understand or if she didn't understand herself.

He wasn't sure it mattered either way. Besides, they had a long life ahead of them and a lot of time to consider the subject further.

Chapter Thirteen

August 24, 1902
San Francisco

Valeria rushed out of the carriage that had ferried her and Francesca back from their painting lesson and flew into the house at full speed, nearly crashing into her father as she headed into the drawing room. Her father let out a hearty laugh.

"Hold on there, young lady, you're likely to hurt yourself or someone else with your running around! Where is it you intend to go at such a speed?"

"Is Mr. Kristiansen with you, Father? Is he out in the garden, perhaps?" Valeria's gaze darted all around the room.

"No, Mr. Kristiansen has taken his leave. You may have noticed his carriage is no longer in the courtyard," Domenico pointed out.

"I never thought to look."

"No, of course not. I must have sympathy for your complete lack of reason when it comes to Mr. Kristiansen. When I have located your mother, perhaps the two of us can persuade you to realign your wits when it comes to this young man."

"Forgive me, Father." Valeria looked sheepishly towards the floor.

Domenico lifted her face towards his with a gentle hand. "There now, let's not be downtrodden. We have much to talk about today."

Valeria brightened. "Do we? Is that why you are looking for Mother?"

"It is indeed. If you will be so good as to seat yourself, I will bring your mother to you, and Francesca as well. It is time for a family meeting."

Valeria watched as her father walked out into the entrance hall. In her restlessness, she strode out into the hall behind him and called for Sergio.

"Sergio, I'm afraid I have lost my sister! Have you seen her come in from the courtyard?"

"I have not, Miss Valeria, but I will be happy to find her if that is your wish," Sergio replied.

"Oh, please do, and ask her to join me in the drawing room at once."

She walked back into the drawing room and settled herself on the loveseat across from her father's favorite chair. She arranged her skirts with the distraction that comes from too much pent-up energy and no appropriate outlet.

Within seconds, Francesca appeared. "Valeria, Sergio told me you wish to see me."

"I do. Father has gone to find Mother and we are all to have a meeting."

"Is that what Father said? Does it concern his meeting with Mr. Kristiansen?" Francesca sat down.

"He did not say, but I do so hope it does." Valeria peered into the foyer, willing her parents to appear so that they could all get on with the matter at hand.

Within minutes, their mother swept into the room and removed the garden hat she had tied securely with a light blue scarf onto the crown of her head. Their father walked behind her and turned abruptly to close the drawing room doors.

"I have interrupted your mother's gardening for this occasion," he said with a smile.

Francesca addressed her mother. "Were you in the greenhouse? Have you seen the orchids?"

"The orchids are in blooming health, Francesca. You have done beautiful work and must be so proud," Adriana confirmed.

"Thank you. It has taken nothing more than restraint on my part. The temptation is to fuss over them, as you know."

"I agree completely. The less you attend to an orchid the better it thrives." She seated herself next to Valeria and placed a comforting hand upon her shoulder. She turned her gaze to her husband as if to say she was now a willing audience.

"Yes, well, now that we are all assembled, I would like to regale you all with the interesting conversation I had with Mr. Kristiansen this afternoon." Her father's gaze darted swiftly from his wife to Francesca, ultimately settling upon Valeria, who could not suppress a spontaneous blush. "Allow me to come straight to the point. Mr. Kristiansen has asked for my permission to marry Valeria."

Valeria's eyes widened, her mother clasped a hand to her chest, and Francesca jumped out of her seat and clapped her hands together with glee.

"Oh, Father, this is wonderful news!" Francesca exclaimed. "You did give your permission, did you not?"

"Now, let's not jump to conclusions, Francesca. Surely you know me better than that. One does not grant one's permission so freely or readily without careful consideration. One has to consider consequences, and I am not in the habit of making rash decisions on any matter, family concerns or otherwise. You do, of course, know that," he reminded her.

"Yes, of course, Father, it was just that—" Francesca began, but Valeria, who had found her voice, searched her father's face for any insight and couldn't withstand the suspense.

"What did you say to him?"

"I said to him what any reasonable man would say. I told Mr. Kristiansen I would consider the matter and send for him on Monday."

Valeria's mother inserted a question. "Did Mr. Kristiansen speak freely about his financial status and his prospects for the future?"

"He did. He volunteered the information quite candidly. It is apparent he has a plan with regard to furthering his already impressive clientele. He means to take his career into his own hands and his reputation beyond the momentum of word-of-mouth. He spoke of advertising in unexplored regions, and what with the stability he currently enjoys, I am convinced that Mr. Kristiansen will have a financially sound future."

"Did you discuss where Mr. Kristiansen would like to live once they are married?" her mother continued.

"We did, but that is a matter I would like to save for later. It is now important that I address Valeria before we go any further." Her father rose from his seat and gestured for Valeria to do the same. He looked searchingly into her eyes. "Tell me, Valeria, is the prospect of a life with Mr. Kristiansen something that attracts or repels you?"

"It thrills me, Father, truly it does," she said without forethought. "I would love to make a life with him and include him into our family. I think it best to speak of this now since we are examining the subject. I have not told you that Mr. Kristiansen has no family of his own."

"Mrs. Davenworth told me as much." Her father's answer surprised them all.

"She did? When was that?" Their mother, caught uncharacteristically off-guard, looked at Valeria and Francesca as if to say, did you know? Both shook their heads quickly and glanced back at their father.

"Mrs. Davenworth, in her own inimitable way, engaged me at our last garden party and presented me with the facts. To hear her speak of Mr. Kristiansen, one would think immediately that the circumstances to which he was born were in his highest interest and we should all be so lucky."

"I think it safe to say Mrs. Davenworth is Mr. Kristiansen's devout champion," Francesca interjected.

"Of course she is, in many ways," their mother added.

"She is very fond of her uncle, Mr. Jorgensen, and it is he who raised Mr. Kristiansen," Valeria offered.

"Yes, I am aware of that." Her father returned to his chair and placed his hands on his knees. He leaned forward for effect and cleared his throat. "Of course, it is of little importance to me whether he has family or not. Norway is far enough away that any family from there would hold a position of non-interference. We all would be doing just as well to consider Mr. Kristiansen as a part of our family."

"Indeed, as it should be," her mother and Francesca

said in unison. Valeria could not hide a slight smile. She liked the vein of the conversation.

"There are future concerns on Mr. Kristiansen's mind that I want him to discuss with Valeria. I want her to know exactly how he envisions their life together so everything is out in the open. Man and wife must be in perfect accord so that there are no surprises and no resentments. Naturally, I have opinions and want to keep a protective arm around Valeria, but ultimately it is her happiness to orchestrate as she will." He looked towards her mother.

"I believe what your father is saying is that you have to look towards the future, Valeria, and what you want the conditions of your life to be. I am referring to subjects such as where you will live, whether or not you desire children, and if so, when. There is also the question of what Mr. Kristiansen expects from you as a wife. The two of you come from very different cultures. It is important that you match minds on how you want to live."

"Yes, Valeria, indeed," Francesca added. "We are fortunate to have progressive-thinking parents. They are not telling you how to live your life. Rather, they are presenting you with questions so that you may come to your own conclusions."

Her mother nodded. "I can always count on you, Francesca. That is precisely my point."

"And my point as well," Valeria's father concurred. "You and Mr. Kristiansen will have a few things to talk over."

"I understand. It is as we have been taught. I am quite capable of thinking for myself, and I am secure in my family's guidance should I ever get into straits. When is it you propose for me to speak with Anders, Father?"

"I will send for him on Monday and leave the two of you unchaperoned, although your mother and I will not be far out of reach. Collect your thoughts between now and then and hear what your young man has to say when he arrives. I will speak to the two of you together at the day's end."

"Thank you, Father, and thank you, Mother. You as well, Francesca. Oh, this is the happiest day of my life. I just know there is nothing but happiness to come!"

Chapter Fourteen

September 21, 1999
Carmel

Three times before, when they were first getting to know each other, Anna and Kevin had made the six-hour drive up the 101 Freeway from Los Angeles to the Monterey Peninsula. Anna had fallen in love with the area upon first sight. She found it mystical, magical, and hauntingly familiar, although she couldn't put her finger on why she felt that way. It was probably the lure of the sea, she mused, the way the air felt clean, yet heavy with mist in the mornings and early evenings, the way the days remained temperate year-round and the nights refreshingly cool. It was as if all of the Monterey Peninsula existed in perpetual fall weather.

Anna told Kevin she felt compatible with the region, that it was their place and she could picture them living there for the rest of their lives. When the decision on where to marry presented itself, Anna concluded it could only be in Carmel-by-the-Sea. For some inexplicable reason, she desperately wanted to marry in Carmel, but how to arrange the logistics without asking their guests to travel? She eventually arrived at a compromise—it would be an intimate ceremony with just the two of them. They could stay in Carmel for the remainder of the week and have a big party when they returned to L.A.

She visualized herself in a long white dress, standing outdoors on a cliff overlooking the sea, with Kevin dressed in a suit, and an officiant to tie the knot. She wanted the two of them to write their own vows, and she would read her favorite poem by William Butler Yeats entitled "He Wishes for the Cloths of Heaven," because it summed up her sentiments word for word. There would be music before and after the ceremony, and she decided a harpist would do quite nicely.

She got on her computer, found an organization called Weddings by the Sea in Carmel, and explained the entire vision to the woman who managed the organization. It was easier to assemble than she imagined, and Anna decided to add to the fun of the entire proceedings by making the details of the ceremony a complete surprise to Kevin.

* * *

Kevin loved the fact Anna had taken charge of their wedding. Although he was a great planner in most respects, he lacked the off-beat creativity that came to Anna naturally. His mother had laughed when he told her Anna would not divulge the specifics of their wedding, and he was grateful to her for not taking offense that their wedding would only include the two of them. His mother had said she would be just as happy to fly out for the party once he and Anna returned to L.A. as a married couple.

In mid-afternoon on the twenty-first of September, Anna and Kevin drove into Carmel-by-the-Sea's town center. It was a mild afternoon, with a light mist in the air, and the pine trees rustled audibly in the breeze.

"Now will you tell me where we're staying?" Kevin brought the Jeep to a stop and looked over at Anna.

"We're staying at the Carriage House Inn on

Junipero, between Seventh and Eighth. It's just a half-block away." She met his gaze.

Kevin engaged the left-hand turn signal and waited for the light to turn green. He pulled into the inn's parking lot, and they both climbed out of the Jeep.

"You stay here, I'll go get the keys," Anna called over her shoulder as she headed toward the inn's office. Within minutes, she returned with a big smile on her face. "This way," she instructed.

They entered a large spacious suite and drifted from room to room. In the living room, Kevin's eyes swept over three towering vases spilling over with flowers and two bottles of champagne cradled in ice. The bedroom contained a warm crackling fire behind a black mesh screen across from the king-size bed, and the bathroom's travertine floor ascended in steps showcasing a Jacuzzi at the apex.

"I think we have all the accoutrements for a successful wedding," Kevin said in mock understatement. "Who sent the flowers?"

"I don't have any idea. Let's look at the cards and see." Anna went to each arrangement and read from its corresponding card. Kevin's parents, Kevin's office, and Lucia had all sent flowers. "See? Everybody's here in spirit! That's just as good as having them here, isn't it?"

"Whatever you say. What about the champagne?"

"Jim Thorpe!" Anna exclaimed.

"Well, I'll be damned. I didn't know he had it in him. I'll have to call him in a minute. What a good guy. He must have recalled he was with me that first night I drove you home from Beverly Hills. That was the beginning of our relationship, remember? I should call him and thank him."

"Let's walk through the town and see what's happening before you do. I feel like moving around after that long drive, but let's go get our luggage first."

After they carried their luggage into the suite, they set out for a walk down Ocean Avenue, which ran through the middle of town with shops and boutiques on either side of the cobblestone sidewalk. By all appearances, Anna seemed to have a destination in mind for her forward stride never faltered.

She came to an abrupt halt in front of Fourtaine Estate Jewelers, where she turned with great flourish and heaved opened the wooden door. The store gleamed with the sparkle of glittering estate jewelry, arranged in counter cases according to variety and set upon tapestry area rugs. Precious gemstones set in gold, white gold, and platinum were designed in filigreed rings, brooches, necklaces, and earrings. Salespeople stood in sophisticated clothing behind spotlighted glass counters. Anna led the way purposefully to the back of the store where a case displaying an array of rubies stood out prominently.

"Hello, we're getting married tomorrow," she said without preamble to the man standing sentry behind the counter. Her eyes swept over the contents of the case. Holding out her left hand, she looked at the salesman. "I'd like to look at a wedding band that complements this engagement ring."

The man smiled. "I'll be happy to assist you."

"I'm Anna and this is Kevin."

"Nice to meet you both, I'm Justin Haines. Are you getting married here in Carmel?"

"Yes, we are. I'd give you the details but then it wouldn't be a surprise for my future husband." Anna beamed.

"I'm just along for the ride." Kevin placed an arm around Anna's shoulder and looked down at the case.

"Can I look at this one?" Anna pointed to a ruby and diamond eternity band. Justin opened the case and placed the ring on a navy blue velvet swatch. She placed the ring on her finger and it fit perfectly. She smiled at Kevin and said, "This is it. This is exactly what I want for a wedding band. It's important that we get it here in Carmel, that's why I asked you to wait. Not only will it commemorate our marriage, it's also going to commemorate the place where we married. That kind of thing means everything to me," she explained.

"Don't you want to look at other rings?" Kevin asked, although he suspected he already knew the answer.

"No, I don't need to, this is definitely it." Anna nodded with certainty.

Kevin lifted her hand for closer inspection. "They do look good together." He picked up an ocular loop and examined the ring at closer range, looking for defects or flaws. When he could find none, he looked at his future wife, amazed at her certainty. Her face was set with determination and told him there was no point in questioning the subject any further.

With all things considered, Kevin did what any man in his position would do—he asked Justin Haines to put the ring in a jeweler's box, pulled out his wallet, and handed him a credit card.

"Well, this woman is easy to please," Justin said with

a laugh. "This is going to be the easiest sale I'll have all year, I can tell already."

"I don't know if it's about Anna being easy to please as much as it's about the fact she knows her own mind and it's not up for negotiation," Kevin offered.

He pocketed the ring, and once out in the street, Kevin said, "I'm not going to let you see this again until the ceremony tomorrow, all right?"

"I promise I won't ask, and anyway the ring isn't going to count until tomorrow, so I'll be good and won't pester you," Anna returned. "Now then, technically, tonight is our rehearsal dinner, and even though we're not going to rehearse, we're still going to make a big deal out of the dinner, okay?"

Anna instructed Kevin to put on a suit and tie then wait for her on the patio while she stole herself away to the bedroom and dressed. When she emerged, she wore a three-quarter-length maroon velvet dress that dipped down in the front and the back. Black satin heels adorned her feet, and a ruby and diamond necklace encased her throat. The diamond stud earrings he had given her on their six-month anniversary set off the necklace nicely, and in her arms she carried a heavy black velvet cape. She looked like she had stepped out of a vintage photograph, which didn't surprise him. He knew she had a deep affinity with the past.

Kevin couldn't help but admire the way the maroon color complemented her jet-black hair and piercing green eyes. He helped her on with her cape and took her by the hand. Together, they crossed Ocean Avenue and turned up Mission Street. They entered a courtyard between Fourth and Fifth Street and walked into a country-French restaurant called Loudas. They dined on trout almandine and drank Puligny-Montrachet wine, the label of which Anna requested to be soaked off the bottle so she could put it in a scrapbook because Anna loved documenting her life. They talked about how happy they were to have found each other and retraced the minute details of how they had met. Anna told him she was sure they were fated to be together.

"This feels like more than fate to me," she said. "It feels like destiny. But it's more than that because everything feels like it's flowing into one and time somehow doesn't enter into the equation."

"So what's the difference between fate and destiny?" Kevin asked.

"I think fate is like the little signposts along the way that point you in the direction of your destiny," Anna explained without pausing. "It seems incredibly right with you, as if my entire life has been leading up to a specific significant moment, like water seeking its own level. You know when it gets there because everything smoothes out and settles in without question or doubt."

"I understand what you're saying. It's as if now that we're together, our lives will really begin."

"Exactly. In a lot of ways, I've been waiting for you."

After dinner, they walked through the misty stillness of Carmel's dark night, their footsteps clicking on the cobblestones as they followed a slope leading down to the sea.

Anna led the way, turning left off Ocean Avenue and veering into the part of Carmel's residential neighborhood where beautiful storybook cottages stood side by side like something in a fairy tale. In the night's stillness, the cottages were luminous—some with shake roofs and stone walls and others with low fences that delineated the yard from the road. The smell of burning wood from a few residential fireplaces hung in the air, and the unlighted street they walked on was deathly quiet save for the soft rustling of wind through the trees. It was a course they'd never taken before and because they walked it at night, it made them cautious, which heightened the intimacy of their solitary nighttime exploration.

They walked onward and turned randomly on Eighth Street, where the road declined dramatically beneath the moving shadows of the half-moon light. On the left, only one block up from the sea, a graceful stone arch loomed at a junction where the road met the sidewalk, heralding an entrance. Anna stood beneath the arch and called Kevin to her side.

"Look at this. Isn't it intriguing? Who knew this hotel was down here?"

"It looks like it's been here for a while." Kevin looked at the structure, its stone pillars carrying the effects of weather-beaten age.

Anna walked through the arch then skirted the side of the hotel until she spied a pair of stone garden benches before the front door. She sat down and looked around her. "Come sit beside me. Let's pretend we live here—that this is really our house.

"This is an ideal location," Kevin observed, sitting down and taking her hand. "I bet this hotel is really old. It also looks expensive."

"It's so quiet around here, it's a little spooky." Anna looked up. "The Madeira Hotel. Isn't that lovely how the name is carved in stone above the doorway? Oh my goodness." She turned. "Look at that window!"

To the left of the door, creating the illusion it was suspended in air since it was lit from within, a large stained-glass window in the shape of a five-pointed star emitted a haunting light. Anna couldn't take her eyes from it and sat down as if spellbound.

"Kevin, does that window remind you of anything?" she finally said.

"I don't know, should it?"

"It's like the painting I made for you of the star. It looks just like it."

"Yes, I see it now," Kevin agreed. "What does this mean?" He smiled at her. "Is this one of your signs? Do you want to stay here because this is a sign?" Kevin, after knowing Anna for so long, was beginning to anticipate her unique way of thinking.

"Maybe it is. I think we should definitely come back and stay here. It's my kind of place. I could do all kinds of pretending here. If we stayed here for a few days, I'd get up in the morning and walk down to the sea as if I lived here and it was part of my daily routine. Can you imagine living here? It would be unreal. Just think how great it would be to live this close to the sea. It would impact every waking moment of our lives. Do you want to walk around? I think we should go exploring," Anna said, though she was already well on her way, walking along the worn red-brick path that led around to the back of the hotel.

They followed the walkway and slowly traced their way through the back gardens, circumnavigating the grounds until they reached the south side of the hotel where a large white-marble fountain splashed sounds into the night. Anna stood transfixed, watching the iridescent marble glow in the moonlight. Following an inexplicable compulsion, she reached out her hand to caress the fountain's smooth surface. "I've always had a thing about fountains, have I ever mentioned that? I swear, it's like a gravitational pull—I'm not exaggerating. We definitely have to come back and stay here. Come over here, come feel this stone, it's almost as smooth as silk."

Kevin stood beside Anna and leaned down, laying his hand on the fountain's basin. "Italian marble."

"How do you know that?"

"Because it's a little soft. You can tell this has been polished and sealed to make it capable of withstanding weather. This fountain was made to stand the test of time."

"I love the way you know about everything." Anna slid her arm around Kevin's waist.

"I know enough to get by," Kevin joked. "What do you want to do now? Do you want to go back to the Carriage House?"

"Not quite yet, let's walk around a little longer."

They walked to the back of the hotel's grounds where a short flight of stone steps led down to the residential road behind the hotel. Veering to the left, they strolled in the darkness under a canopy of ancient pine trees, following the symphonic cacophony of breaking waves filtering forth from the night sea. Off to the right, a gravel path leading down to the sand caught Anna's attention and beckoned her forward.

Bending down, she took off her shoes and held them

in her right hand while her left hand swept her long hair to the side and caught the top of her cape against the rising wind. She moved lightly, her bare feet scarcely breaking the surface of the crusted sand, and marched headlong to the water's edge. She stood stock still, casting her gaze into the darkness looming over the metallic sea. After a moment, she turned and folded herself into Kevin's warm chest, gathering him in a tight embrace.

"Hold me tighter. Can you feel our lives beginning already?"

"Yes, and tomorrow we'll be married." Kevin held her closer. "Tomorrow we will really begin."

Chapter Fifteen

August 26, 1902
San Francisco

At five-thirty in the afternoon, Sergio answered the Siennas' front door and ushered Anders into the drawing room where Domenico Sienna waited.

"You are always impressively punctual, Mr. Kristiansen," Domenico began, "so in honor of your good manners, let me get right to the point. Valeria waits for you in the eastern garden, and I trust you will want to have a word with her regarding your proposal. After you have done so, I would like to speak to the two of you together."

"It will be my pleasure, sir." Anders slipped a hand into his coat pocket and patted the ring that lay inside. He stepped out onto the brick walkway that led to the eastern garden and found Valeria holding a parasol that shielded her fair skin from the rays of the fading sun. He walked confidently forward until he reached her side.

"Well, I have come at last," Anders said.

Valeria looked up, with a blush staining her cheeks, and a welcoming smile. "You have at that. Shall we sit down and enjoy the remainder of the afternoon?"

"Yes, and let us talk about the future." He sat down on the garden bench and drew her by the hand beside him. When he turned to face her, the words spilled unbidden from his lips. "I know your father has spoken to you of my intentions."

"My father and I have no secrets between us," Valeria returned.

"Then I shall ask you directly how you would view the subject of marriage in general, and specifically how you would consider the subject of marriage to me." Anders looked at her intently.

"I am glad you have phrased your question as such. I think it most important to discuss the subject of marriage generally before we discuss it specifically," she answered.

"Very well, then. What is your general vision of a happy marriage between a man and a woman?"

"My general vision is similar to what I have seen in my own parents' marriage. I see two people very much in love who respect and complement each other. They aspire to the same kind of lifestyle wherein they place great importance on family and friendships. My mother supports my father in a way that encourages his financial success, for she takes a keen interest in his business dealings. He, in turn, celebrates her creative pursuits.

"It is about the little things, really, such as my mother's gardening interests, her love of entertaining, her joy in making our home beautiful, and how she has lovingly raised their four children. My father sees immense value in everything she does. She is encouraged to arrange her life as she sees fit, and because my father is a willing supporter, my mother spends most of her time arranging his happiness. It is a formula of balance and success."

"I readily see how it would be a formula for success. Now then, what of your interests?"

"I also have an interest in gardening as well as

painting. Mind you, I am not in the same league with you, but I do love the art. Francesca and I both inherited that from our mother. I, too, like the idea of creating a beautiful home and of entertaining friends and family. I consider myself well qualified for both."

"And the raising of children, where your mother excels so brilliantly, what do you think of that?"

"I look forward to the day when I can do the same for my children as my mother has done for all of us. She is a strong disciplinarian but it comes from a respect for manners and civility. She gives us room to make our own decisions, but if they vary greatly from her views, she has a way of guiding us towards a better way of thinking."

Anders nodded. "I understand."

Valeria turned the tables. "And you? What do you think a happy marriage entails?"

"I think it is just as you described. I can neither add nor detract a thing. I can see your character assets, I recognize they have risen from your upbringing, and I sincerely admire them. I am a simple man with one focus outside of you and that is my painting career. When it comes to matters of domesticity, I think these things are safest left in the hands of women. Of the two genders, women are by far the more qualified."

"And children?" Valeria prodded.

"For obvious reasons, I want to give my own children everything I never had."

"Are you speaking of your childhood?" Valeria looked at him with what seem to be tenderness.

"Yes, I am." Anders averted his gaze from Valeria's face. He had to choose his words wisely. "Valeria, when one thinks of an orphan, they usually picture a wayward, unfortunate little child with nothing to tether him to normalcy. That was not the case with me. I am one of the lucky ones, all because of Lars Jorgensen. He was everything to me from the age of six that a doting father could be. He was my father, my mentor, and my confidant, so you see, I do in fact have a foundation of stability. When I say I want to give my children everything I never had, what I mean specifically is actual family. There is very little beyond that because it is the only thing I have lacked. I did know love, security, comfort, and respect, and once again, I am one of the lucky ones."

"Thank you for explaining. I think I do understand, Anders. You are an optimist and rather than cursing your fate, you have chosen to see only the good that came from your relationship with Mr. Jorgensen. Oh, how I would love to meet the man."

"And meet him you shall, if you will have me, Valeria. There is one other thing I would like to discuss with you."

"Very well." Valeria looked expectantly at him.

He hoped she would be open-minded. He raked a hand through his hair—a gesture he habitually performed when nervous. "It is a subject which you have already broached, and it is, quite pointedly, the subject of your home."

Anders paused and gathered himself. He began again. "As I look towards my future, most importantly I see you with me, and secondly, I see us both surrounded by incomparable beauty." He turned and looked searchingly into her eyes. "I hope you recall the landscape painting at my studio. I recall you looking at it and remarking upon its beauty. It is, as I told you, a scene depicting the coastal area of Carmel on the Monterey Peninsula. I would like us to live there. I would like to build you a house and have it be everything you ever wanted. I know it is asking much of you to consider living apart from your family, but as I told your father, Carmel is less than a four and a half hour train ride from here, and please think of the wonderful visits we all could have."

Anders studied Valeria's face for a reaction, yet found nothing discernible. He continued his line of reasoning, hoping to plead his case. "I am inspired by the region, which will surely enhance my work. Carmel is a young town, and we are young people. I can only see the compatibility in that happenstance. You and I could grow with the town and make our way together amongst like-minded people in a thriving artistic community. I think it would be absolutely ideal."

Valeria looked into Anders' eyes. "I will gladly go where you go."

He pulled the box from his pocket, removed the ring with remarkable steadiness, and placed it on Valeria's left hand. She looked down at the emerald-cut diamond set in platinum and smiled.

"Do you like it?" Anders asked sincerely.

"I love it. It's the most gorgeous thing I've ever seen. I'll love it forever," she said breathlessly.

"Will you do me the honor of becoming my wife?"

"I will." She smiled. "Let me just sit here with you and prolong the moment, then we'll go inside and speak with my father."

Chapter Sixteen

September 22, 1999
Carmel

Anna stood before the full-length mirror in the bedroom of the Carriage House Inn and looked at the small wreath in her hand made from fresh wildflowers. The Village Florist shop had delivered the wreath earlier that morning, and at the time Anna thought it would look nice upon her head. She fingered the white satin ribbon flowing from the back of the wreath and although it was lovely, she decided it looked more like part of a costume from a Renaissance faire than a headpiece for a wedding.

She placed the wreath on the dresser and walked back to the mirror. Picking up her brush, she fanned her hair before her and began to stroke downward until it gleamed in the late afternoon sun. She pushed her hair behind her so it would fall halfway down her back instead of obstructing the view of the front of her dress. The sleeveless ivory-colored silk was understated and simple, save for the sheer organza drape that fell from the back of the dress. She took the material and lifted her arms outward, letting the drape float down like descending mist. When she had first seen the dress, the drape reminded her of a delicate cape, and Anna considered how it would drift behind her if the wind was just right on the cliff overlooking Carmel Bay.

She caught her breath, realizing the time was now

upon her. In a moment Kevin would walk through the door, and they would begin the journey to the cliffs where the Justice of the Peace waited.

* * *

Kevin looked at his watch for the second time in five minutes. He stood out on the sidewalk before the Carriage House, biding his time because Anna had said it was bad luck to see her dress until the very last minute. He decided to walk the streets of downtown Carmel in order to give Anna private time to dress, and hoped it would ward off his building anxiety. Why, he wondered, did he feel the conflicting surges of anxiety and anticipation at the same time? After what he considered a reasonable amount of time, he started back to the Carriage House. When he reached the door to their suite, he stopped for a moment, deciding it best to knock.

"This feels like a first date," he said when Anna opened the door, then he took a step backwards, giving her wide berth to come outside. "Nice dress. You look stunning," he said in a voice that seemed understated compared to the emotion welling up inside.

"Do you like it? I'm so glad." Anna twirled around. "What about the cape?"

Kevin smiled. "Nice touch."

"And you, my dear, look splendid. Since both of us look like we're dressed for a wedding, what do you say we go get married?"

"Right this way." Kevin unlocked the Jeep and held open the passenger door while Anna gathered her full-length dress and carefully climbed inside.

The Justice of the Peace greeted them at the head of the path leading to the cliffs overlooking Carmel Bay. She was a tall, stately woman who wore a conservative suit, and she held out a clip-board instructing Anna and Kevin to sign the marriage certificate before they started the ceremony. Once completed, they walked the path to their wedding site, where an Irish harpist sat tuning his instrument. A steady breeze lifted his shoulder-length hair, and he stood up abruptly when he saw Anna and Kevin approach.

"You hired a harpist?" Kevin laughed, and Anna could see he was pleasantly surprised.

"No wedding is complete without a harpist."

"Or without a photographer," came a voice from behind. Anna turned and smiled into the eyes of a tall young man holding a tripod and a Leica camera.

"I think we're ready to begin," Anna proclaimed.

* * *

The ceremony was not a long one, but it contained all the elements of which Anna had dreamed. Music created ambience before and after they exchanged their vows. Anna read the Yeats poem, the photographer documented the highlights, and Kevin held her hand all throughout the poignant ceremony. She stood high upon a cluster of large boulders, her pink ballet shoes allowing her to feel the stone beneath her feet. Although the feel of the stone grounded her while she looked into Kevin's eyes, she felt an accompanying sense of timelessness as the wind blew her hair around her shoulders.

Something seemed oddly familiar, almost like déjà vu. Everything felt reminiscent of something she had known before, yet it lay ephemeral and dreamlike in the back of her mind. She could not put the feeling into words but she could feel her soul take a sigh of relief as she recognized she had finally come home.

Chapter Seventeen

June 22, 1903 – April 10, 1904
San Francisco

Valeria and Anders had searched out her father to tell him of their plans to marry.

"Your mother will have a field day," he'd said, embracing the pair of them.

His words were true; her mother was in her element for every moment of the pre-wedding months because she was a great organizer, list maker, and delegator. She took immediate charge and began the wedding preparations by assembling a list of things that would absolutely not take place before or during the ceremony, for she was a superstitious woman and she wanted to rule out entirely the possibility of creating any bad luck for Valeria and Anders.

"I want to give you every advantage I can think of," she said to Valeria, "for how you begin your marriage will set the stage for the years to follow. Some things are not merely superstitions, you know. There are truths to many of the ceremonial traditions that have survived. I am not one to tempt fate, so we're going to adhere to many of the rules. To begin with, I will not consider holding the wedding on any other day of the week than Wednesday. The old saying goes: 'Monday is for wealth, Tuesday is for health, Wednesday the best day of all. Thursday for crosses, Friday for losses, Saturday no luck at all.' Sunday, of course, is the Lord's day, so we have no other option than Wednesday if we are going to start your marriage off with good fortune."

"Of course, Mother," Valeria conceded.

"It will be a late-morning garden wedding with Father Santiago officiating, and I am thinking your young man will want to wear a formal frock coat and top hat. I'll have a word with him about that. Frock coats are still the fashion, and we'll have to organize his colors so they complement the bridal party. His waist coat can be white to match your dress, but we'll have to decide on either blue or perhaps a wine color for the rest."

"I'll see that he speaks with you well ahead of time," Valeria agreed.

"Please do, and we'll have to send for the seamstress immediately to start on your dress. There is no such thing as getting started too early. I'm sure you know that you may not breathe a word of your dress to Anders before the ceremony."

"I do know that, nor may I let him see me in it, nor may I stand before a mirror and look at myself in it before the ceremony."

"No, it is bad luck for you to look at yourself in the mirror wearing your full wedding attire, but there is a convenient way around that."

"How so?" Valeria couldn't imagine.

"You simply leave a glove off, or perhaps a shoe, so that you are not completely dressed. Now then, we have something old, something new, something borrowed, but we have to decide upon something blue. The color blue will protect you against bad luck or unhappiness. I would suggest a blue garter, but I want you to wear the one my mother gave to me for my wedding, and it is pink."

"I would love to wear the garter you wore. We'll think of something blue, don't worry, Mother," Valeria assured her. She was amused at her mother's list of traditions and superstitions but she decided to blindly follow on the off-chance Adriana might be right.

Valeria, her mother, and Francesca scrutinized the details of the wedding for months. They discussed the flowers—whose names could only begin with one of the letters in Anders' first name—and the cake, which would be cut into slivers narrow enough to pass through a ring. The cake would be distributed to unmarried female guests so that they could put it under their pillows at night and dream of their future husbands. They decided upon the marquee tent for the reception and chose hanging baskets of trailing flowers and ivy to wrap around each pole. The buffet would be simple, consisting of finger sandwiches, canapés, fresh fruit tarts, pastries, champagne, claret wines, and assorted teas.

Francesca took charge of all the flowers and met with floral designers in San Francisco regarding decorating the marquee and the interior of the house, as well as tending its exterior to ensure the gardens surrounding the house were at their best. Her mother hired the wait staff, took charge of the guest list, hired a string quartet along with a harpist, and oversaw a budget approved by Valeria's father. Valeria concerned herself with her eight bridesmaids, their dresses, and the construction of her own. As the April wedding day approached, the staff in the Sienna household doubled so that some could manage mundane daily affairs while others focused entirely upon the wedding.

When the day of the wedding arrived, the doorbell rang at eight in the morning and into the Sienna household walked Mrs. Fitzgerald, the seamstress, with her two daughters, equally as dedicated to the affair. They carried Valeria's wedding dress and shoes and were shown into the upstairs quarters where Valeria waited nervously. After kissing Valeria on the cheek, Francesca left and made her way into the servants' quarter of the house, where the other seven bridesmaids were dressing.

Valeria wished her mother would appear. Her skin tingled with nerves, and her mother's presence always calmed her. She looked at the clock on the mantel and hoped it wouldn't take the full two hours to assemble her wedding attire. She wondered if Anders was as nervous as she was, then decided he couldn't possibly be, for he was very much a self-assured man.

The youngest of the Fitzgerald daughters spread Valeria's veil over two large chairs, preparing for its attachment to the headdress. The girl looked at her mother for approval and received a short nod as Mrs. Fitzgerald continued to fluff the skirt of Valeria's dress. The elder daughter lifted a pair of shoes from a white box tied with a silver ribbon. They were not of the lace-up variety, which were popular, but looked like fragile hand-sewn ballet slippers. Valeria touched their pink satin ribbons and thought they were the most feminine shoes she had ever seen.

Her mother entered the room just as Valeria held her arms overhead. Mrs. Fitzgerald stood on a stool, holding the wedding dress at an angle that made it easier to lower onto Valeria's shoulders. With its long sleeves and paper-lace cuffs, the dress was an ivory color that buttoned intricately up the back until it culminated in a high lace collar. The satin skirt, covered in the same lace, created the overall illusion that the dress was lighter than air.

Valeria turned towards her mother once her dress was arranged. Their eyes met and they smiled at the same time. In her right hand, her mother carried a small black velvet pouch from which she pulled a string of pearls and a cameo brooch. Valeria turned around, and her mother pinned the brooch on her collar and hooked the necklace around her neck. Inviting her to sit down before the vanity mirror, her mother took a silver-handled brush and began to brush Valeria's hair. She pulled it straight back and twisted it into a chignon which she fastened with silver and ivory combs. When the task was completed, Mrs. Fitzgerald attached Valeria's headdress and its veil cascaded regally down her back.

"The guests have been arriving for the past half-hour. It won't be long now," her mother informed them.

"And Anders?" Valeria whispered anxiously.

"Mr. Kristiansen is scheduled to be the last to arrive. I am certain his carriage will be here perfectly on time with him smiling broadly, for this is the most important day of his life."

* * *

Anders wanted to arrive an enthusiastic hour earlier than the designated time, but the socially conscious Lars Jorgensen, who had arrived in town for the wedding the night before, counseled against the notion. Lars did most everything according to etiquette, and although twenty-six and old enough to decide things for himself, Anders acquiesced with little resistance.

Lars Jorgensen secured his pocket-watch. "This is the bride's day," he reminded Anders. "No sense in loitering about the premises looking impatient in your black frock coat when your presence will not be required for another hour and a half. We wouldn't want to deprive your bride of her anticipation, would we?"

Lars, a catalyst in Anders' life, was the brother of Mrs. Davenworth's father, whose family hailed from the northern region of Trondelag in central Norway. The Jorgensens were members of rural Norwegian society and were landowning farmers who had made a sizeable income from their timberlands. In his early twenties, Lars had decided to leave the central region and make his way to the big city of Trondheim to study law. After five years, he set up an independent law practice and seamlessly became a member of the city's finest society circles.

He married a beautiful socialite by the name of Elsa Eindride and was blissfully happy until Elsa tragically died in childbirth along with their baby four and a half years after their marriage. With neither a wife nor an heir, desolately heartbroken and seeking substance in his life, Lars threw himself further into his law practice. He took on an overwhelming amount of work that gave him cause to affiliate with a wider sphere of activity, which came to include a local orphanage. It was there Lars first came into contact with Anders Kristiansen.

He took notice of the six-year-old boy when he heard the orphanage had designed a new room dedicated to art and recreation. Curious about the new addition, he wandered into the quarters, where he found Anders hunched over a strong coarse cloth drawing an outline in charcoal.

"My mother is an artist," Lars said to Anders. "I try my hand at pastels myself. Do you ever use color?"

Anders looked up, his interest in the subject overshadowing his apprehension of the elegant stranger peering over his shoulder. "No, sir. We have nothing here except black chalk."

As the story was told to Anders later in life, Lars felt his heart crack open, and his recent loss, compounded by his oppressive grief as he took in the child's measure, gave him cause to evaluate his life's stock. Both of his parents were alive; he had an older brother in Trondelag who was married with two children; and although grateful for his family, Lars had nothing specific he could call his own. He went to the rectory and offered a suggestion. It started with monthly visits, and before long Lars had an entire area in his living room transformed for the purpose of creating works of art. He amassed canvases, mixing boards, paints, and colored chalk. On the third Saturday of each month, he rode out to the orphanage to collect Anders, for nothing in his life took precedence over their monthly visit.

Before long, their visits evolved into a weekly rhythm where the two would paint side-by-side. Lars shared everything he knew about drawing until it became clear Anders had surpassed everything he could offer in the way of tutelage. Lars knew a local art historian who suggested a weekend art school for Anders, but Anders could not attend the school while he lived in the orphanage. Lars went back to the orphanage and legally adopted Anders, proposing to be his mentor as well as his legal guardian. It was the easiest decision of Lars' life. It brought a sense of purpose and dedication to each of their lives, and both Anders and his mentor flourished in the other's jurisdiction.

Lars Jorgensen was a visionary man who liked to bring out the best in people. No matter how unusual a person's attributes appeared to be, he knew how to foster them, so when he arrived at the conclusion his adopted son had a natural talent for drawing, rather than being dismayed he set about the business of laying a foundation for his further development.

He sent Anders to a private boys' school in Trondheim for his formal education, as well as the weekend art school his friend had recommended. He also saw to it that Anders' extra-curricular activities ingratiated him into the local art scene. Together they visited art shows and gallery openings, and Anders was introduced about town as an accomplished painter. At first, interested parties came to view his work at home, but it wasn't long before Anders had his own shows. His reputation grew when he evolved from a landscape painter to a portrait artist, and he was the only good one anywhere in the vicinity.

Word spread, and by the time Anders turned twenty-four, a portrait of his hung in every home of significance in Trondheim. Lars had been immensely proud of his accomplishments and boasted to his family in Trondelag, who of course sent word to Cornelia Davenworth in America, and with everyone's blessing, Anders set sail for San Francisco—all at the orchestration of Lars Jorgensen.

"Well now, here we are on the morning of your marriage. Who could have anticipated when you set sail for America that this would happen so quickly? Fate, I suppose, has its own agenda, but I am happy to report I was well prepared for this."

Anders smiled. "Well prepared? Were you well prepared by only three letters from me?"

"It was that which opened the door to the idea, but it was Domenico Sienna who walked through it and made me well aware of your intentions," Lars informed him.

Anders could not have been more surprised, and the look on his face confirmed his astonishment.

"Surely this does not come as a surprise to you. You have not made the mistake of underestimating Domenico Sienna, have you?"

"Perhaps I have not grasped the full range of his scope."

"Then I will inform you. The first time I heard from Domenico Sienna was on the day you sent your calling card to his daughter. He sent word to me by telegraph. It was quite an event for me. His was the first telegram I have ever received."

"But how— " Anders began, but Lars cut him off.

"Cornelia Davenworth, of course. Domenico Sienna has a talent for going straight to the source. Speaking of whom, I expect we'll be seeing him momentarily."

"Mr. Sienna? Here?" For the second time in less than one minute, Anders could not have been more surprised.

"Yes. The two of us want a quick word with you," Lars added.

Anders did not anticipate this meeting with pleasure, but Lars was neither asking for his permission nor his approval. He looked closely at his mentor and thought he saw a mischievous look in his eyes.

The clatter of horses' hooves sounded on the drive before Anders' cottage, and out of the carriage sprang Domenico Sienna, who walked with a sense of entitlement straight into the room in which Lars and Anders were standing.

"Mr. Jorgensen, at last we meet." Domenico extended his hand. "Anders." Domenico nodded towards him. "Lovely day for a wedding, is it not? No rain or clouds in sight. It is all a good omen, my wife tells me."

Anders didn't know whether to prepare himself for a speech, a lecture, or scrutiny in general, but he offered the two men a seat while he gathered his wits.

Domenico preferred to stand, which made his unannounced presence all the more intimidating, and reaching into his waistcoat, he theatrically produced a set of folded papers and handed it to Anders.

"I am a man who takes men at their word," he looked at Anders, "and seeing as how I have a vested interest in your word, Mr. Jorgensen and I have taken the liberty of acting on your behalf."

Anders looked at both men and carefully unfolded the papers.

"It is our gift to you and your bride," Lars added.

Anders leaped to his feet the instant it registered that what he held in his hands was the deed to five acres of land in Carmel, California.

* * *

The wedding of Valeria Sienna to Anders Kristiansen was the social event of the season and the guests came from far and wide. Valeria's two brothers sailed in for the wedding from Italy. Domenico's brother and his family took the train from Los Angeles after their sail from Naples. Adriana's sister and brother-in-law made the journey all the way from Pennsylvania, bringing their two young children to serve as Valeria's attendants.

One hundred and twenty-five local guests had been invited and every one of them came. The ceremony surpassed everyone's expectations. The sight of Valeria on Domenico Sienna's arm as they emerged from the entrance hall of the house and descended the lawn's white-marble stairs to where Father Santiago waited in his vestment alongside Anders and Lars Jorgensen was something that set a new standard for future society weddings.

Eight bridesmaids dressed in lavender preceded Valeria, having come in the wake of two rose petal-throwing children who carried wicker baskets and ambled awkwardly and self-consciously upon a lavender-colored tarpaulin. Father Santiago looked splendid in his ceremonial vestment, with the bridesmaids positioned to his left. Valeria handed her bouquet of white roses to Francesca and placed a light hand on Anders' waiting arm, while Domenico stepped to the right and stood beside Lars. It was a solemn and reverent ceremony with a spectacular group of guests all dressed in their finery surrounding the bridal party.

The sky was blue, the air was soft, and when the official ceremony concluded, Anders looked at Valeria and could tell she was emotionally overwhelmed. When he bent towards her to kiss her for the first time as man and wife, Valeria kept her eyes open wide and so did he.

* * *

Music filled the air as the wedding party disbanded and flowed upon the decorated lawn where a luncheon banquet awaited. Mrs. Davenworth sashayed to Lars' side and, with a tilt of her refined head, looked up into his smiling eyes. "Well, there it is, Uncle. Our young man's fate has taken a new turn, and I cannot express my joy emphatically enough."

Lars whole-heartedly agreed, saying, "And I, Cornelia, am indebted to you for your role in this as well. I look back now and realize destiny has been at play all along and I too could not be more pleased."

Domenico spied the pair of them and approached. "You two look conspiratorial. As the father of the bride, I demand to be privy."

"Now then, Domenico," Cornelia reprimanded, "allow us foreigners to bask in our good fortune. They make a lovely match and it requires very little imagination to envision the adorable grandchildren they will give you and my dear uncle."

"You sound like my Adriana, Cornelia. You women are always on to the next step." Domenico laughed.

"We are exactly that," Mrs. Davenworth agreed and, turning to her right, she extended her arm to include Adriana Sienna who hurriedly approached.

"I thought I heard the mention of grandchildren."

"You did," Domenico confirmed, putting an arm around his wife's waist.

"Lars has told me that the young couple will be moving south to Carmel," Cornelia said to Adriana. "You will miss them, I am sure."

"It will be a test of her restraint, no doubt." Domenico smiled. "Adriana and I both will have to trust that these young ones can be left to their own devices without any harm coming to them."

"I am sure it will take every ounce of fortitude you can muster, but I cannot help but point out that you will have assistance. I know Valeria and Francesca are close, and seeing as how Francesca is still single, you can send her as your emissary," Mrs. Davenworth said.

"Indeed we shall," Adriana concurred. "My prayer is that no harm comes to any of them while they are out of my reach. One always feels a measure of insecurity with one's children so far away. Funny thing about being a parent, it appears one is never truly at peace with the idea of letting them go into the waters of life on their own without supervision."

"That, my dear, is where a leap of faith becomes necessary," Domenico said. "We must all be patient with my dear wife, she is the superstitious sort. I believe what she means by the waters of life is anything that happens without her knowledge!"

Lars raised his glass in a toast. "Here's to the mother of the bride."

"Hear, hear," Domenico and Cornelia joined in heartily.

* * *

When the wedding festivities of what was clearly the social event of the season died down, Valeria descended from the upstairs quarters, dressed in her going-away outfit. Anders stood poised at the front door, prepared to open it, so that the two could walk hand in hand into the throng of rice-throwing well-wishers. He paused before he opened the door, took her face in his hands, and kissed her firmly on her lips.

"And now, my love," he said, "we shall begin."

Chapter Eighteen

September 22, 2000
Carmel

Anna stood looking at the four dresses she'd brought to Carmel for the weekend. She always over-packed because she liked to have a choice. "If you won't tell me where we're going, how will I know how to dress?" She tried to pry the information out of Kevin.

"Now you know how it feels. If memory serves, you did something similar to me just last year on our wedding day. In fact, you were mysterious for an entire week. It's not fun being left in the dark, is it?"

"Okay, okay, I get it. You're paying me back an exact year to the day—fair play. I had no idea you were so good at keeping score. Now will you please tell me where we're going?"

"Absolutely not, but wear your nicest dress."

Anna pulled her short black sleeveless dress from the armoire and produced a pair of black pumps from the closet floor. She stalked into the bathroom for dramatic effect and haughtily closed the door. She let out an immediate laugh when she spotted an ice bucket with an opened bottle of champagne on the counter beside two champagne glasses. She poured two glasses, opened the door, and smiled at Kevin. "Am I that predictable?" She handed him a glass.

"Only predictable when you're irritated." Kevin took the glass from her. "Now hurry up and get ready."

They stepped out into the night and started walking through Carmel's residential neighborhood on their way to the center of town.

"I bet we're going to Little Napoli," Anna guessed.

Kevin laughed. "Wrong restaurant, but it's on the way. Keep walking."

After three additional blocks, they took a left where Kevin stopped abruptly. A delighted smile touched her lips when she realized they stood before the French Poodle. "The same restaurant we went to on our wedding night! I should have guessed," she exclaimed.

Kevin held open the door, and Anna glided into the dark, romantic restaurant. The same waiter who had served them on their wedding night greeted them at the door and led them to their table. Christopher remembered them both.

"Right this way, Mr. and Mrs. Townsend," he said respectfully.

"Nice to see you again, Christopher, how is your wife?" Anna sat down in the chair he pulled out for her.

Christopher looked curiously from Anna to Kevin. "I don't believe I'd even asked her to marry me when I saw you last, but my wife is fine, thank you. We've been married for three months now."

"That's wonderful! So now you're happily married?" Anna smiled up at him.

"Just like the two of you. Happy anniversary. May I offer you anything to start?"

"We'll have a bottle of Puligny-Montrachet." Kevin looked at Anna, who nodded her approval. Christopher excused himself to retrieve the wine.

Kevin leaned forward in his chair. "Anna, how did

you know he got married?"

"I don't know, it just came to me," she said nonchalantly.

"Well, it's nice to know that your antennae are up. Is there anything else I need to know since you're being psychic, or is that it?"

"I'll let you know if there's anything else."

"You mean you'll let me know *when* there's something else."

"Only if I think you should know." She reached across the table and squeezed his hand.

After dinner, they walked leisurely through the streets of town, taking aimless detours up every side street that caught their fancy. They had spent three hours at the French Poodle and it was well past eleven at night. The streets were misty and desolate save for the occasional couple walking hand in hand, making their way towards home. The shop windows and art galleries were ghostly silent, illuminated from within by interior lights.

They took their time looking through windows where oil-painted landscapes and seascapes of the area were positioned in muted gold frames. They looked so real that Anna stood mesmerized before a swirling portrayal of Carmel Bay.

"Look at this one, "she said to Kevin and gestured. "You can tell it's Carmel Bay at sunset even though there's nothing in it but moving water and only the hint of white sand. The artist captured a mood. Strange to look closely and realize the arrangement of seven different colors can affect a mood so completely, don't you think? I am emotionally affected by this—almost physically affected."

"Good art is always evocative, especially for someone as sensitive as you. I bet this makes you feel as if you're standing on Carmel Bay."

"It seriously does," she said as an idea came to her. Not wanting to put an end to the night and feeling safe in the arms of Carmel's tranquil environment, Anna took Kevin's hand and steered him to Ocean Avenue.

"I know it's late, but let's walk down to the water's edge like we did the night before we were married. You don't mind, do you?"

"Whatever you want to do."

"I want to find that same path we took to the sand last year. I think I know where it is. It's not far from the hotel."

"Okay, I'll let you lead. We can do the exact same thing we did last year if you want to, it'll be like a reenactment."

They crossed Ocean Avenue at Dolores, acutely aware that they were the only people walking through the dark residential neighborhood at that hour. They turned right at Eighth Street and started downhill, neither saying a word until Kevin broke the silence.

"I think we did everything right for our wedding, don't you? I mean, you're not sorry it was just the two of us, are you? Should we have invited your sister to the wedding?"

"No, it was perfect, and anyway, Lucia never likes to go to coastal areas. I've never understood why. She prefers being inland instead, places like the desert or the mountains, that kind of thing. For some reason, Lucia is afraid of water. Anyway, we made the right decision by not asking people to travel. I think we did everything right."

The wind grew stronger as they made their way seaward and the lights from the neighborhood faded behind them. They crossed the lane behind the Madeira Hotel and continued south until the little path appeared at the right.

"This is it!" Anna began walking the path, though it was pitch-dark and the mist from the sea thickened the air.

Suddenly Anna stopped and looked expectantly behind her. She thought she'd sensed movement just over her shoulder, yet when she turned all she noticed were the swaying limbs of the trees overhead.

"There's something about this little path," she eventually said. "Doesn't it seem like this is a path locals have used for generations? There's something about the angle of it, I don't know how to explain it. It doesn't seem to be a well-traveled path now, but it feels as if once upon a time this was the obvious way to get down to the sea."

She looked about. "There's nothing around here except for these ancient massive trees and the shadows they cast, but still, it feels almost populated to me," she continued. "I feel a little spooked. By any chance, do you feel like you're being watched? I do."

The roar of the waves precluded any response Kevin could have made, so he put his arm around her shoulders and pulled her in close. They stood where the lane joined the sand and listened to the tide as they looked towards the sea. A half-moon lit the sky, casting silver upon the darkened water.

Anna inhaled and let the mood move through her, straining to employ all her senses. She wanted to exist fully in the moment. She took in the sound of the surf, the darkness of the sky, the subtle glow of the sand, and the salty moisture that enveloped them. A disturbing feeling crept over her, suggesting there was something she had forgotten.

She scanned her memory. It felt like something she had known in a dream, and she tried to identify its significance. Pulling her coat a little tighter, she turned to Kevin and spoke as if he already knew what she was thinking.

"I cannot recall what I'm supposed to remember," she said, but the air was so thick it drowned out her words.

Kevin took Anna's hand and started walking back in the direction of the Madeira Hotel—the damp making her even colder. They walked back up the path and turned left, taking the road that eased up behind the hotel's garden. They stepped onto the brick sidewalk leading to their room, but Anna continued walking onwards, bypassing their room's door.

"Follow me for just a minute," she whispered.

They walked to the hotel's back door and found it open. Quietly, they slipped inside. The lobby looked larger without any people about, and the dim lighting divided the room into sections where pools of light fell from tabletop lamps, leaving other areas darkened in contrast. Anna crept forward silently, and without breaking stride, she walked until her hand reached the wrought-iron rail of the front stairs. So quick was her forward momentum, it left Kevin behind.

In that moment, her desire to move forward outweighed the fact she walked alone in the dark, but she continued, possessed with a certainty that something important awaited her at the top of the stairs. Once on the top step, her gaze instinctively turned towards an open window where a light from the garden radiated below. She stepped to the window, put a hand to its glass, and stroked downward as if reacquainting herself with the texture. Longing welled up inside her, nostalgia for a time she could not quite recall.

Suppressing the need to sigh, a vision grew from her mind's eye as she turned cautiously to her left. In the core of her being, she felt somebody was watching her. A chill rippled on the surface of her skin, and a knot appeared in her solar plexus traveling straight for her throat, constricting it as if trying to control the need to scream. Her vision tripped in and out of focus, and although she felt lightheaded, she held her head high and willed herself to look towards the end of the hall.

A closed wooden door loomed heavily before her, and she approached it, knowing in her bones that behind it lay a master bedroom. With trepidation, she took six steps forward until her vision blurred completely. She felt almost faint so she shook her head. When her vision cleared, she looked forward and saw herself standing in the master bedroom before a large bay window, looking fretfully towards the sea.

How could that be?

How could she, simultaneously, be watching *herself* and experiencing what she was experiencing? Overwhelmed and terrified, she felt as if the past and the present were colliding right before her eyes.

Tree branches scratched against the window pane, and the branches partially obscured the vision of what she perceived to be a woman running frantically towards the house. The woman held her long skirts in her hands and ran at a fevered pace. She was somebody Anna knew; she was somebody Anna remembered.

Fear gripped her and she strained her eyes, the better to focus, but the attempt drained her. She became suddenly aware she stood frozen in place by a fear that wanted to bring her to her knees.

Chapter Nineteen

September, 1907
Carmel

In the three years since her marriage, Valeria had grown from a sheltered girl of nineteen to confident mistress of her own household. She took pride in her newly acquired autonomy, and everything from her home to her circle of friends reflected who she was with her own personal style.

The house Anders commissioned for them was not a large one, but it stood on five acres of land with a view of the sea and already there were plans for expansion. Partially fashioned in the popular architectural style of the region, the two-story house resembled a Spanish mission with stucco walls, Carmel sandstone floors, plenty of windows, and unique wrought-iron fixtures. Her husband had thought to add Italian-style features such as high ceilings and wall sconces because he knew it would please Valeria. A heavy wooden front door faced the sparsely populated residential street, and beside the door a star-shaped stained-glass window looked out on the street from halfway up the staircase in the foyer. Behind the house, a spacious garden crowned with a white-marble fountain similar to the one Valeria had grown up with sat on a knoll facing the sea.

She spent most of her days tending to the running of their house, for there was always work to be done within and without its four sturdy walls.

They employed a delightful Irish couple: Bridget, who cooked and cleaned on Monday, Wednesday, and Friday, and her husband Jimmy, who took care of the grounds. The task of overseeing them fell to Valeria, and she fulfilled her role as mistress of the house joyfully with a specific vision for how everything should be. She wanted to ensure that every aspect of their house reflected their backgrounds, talents, and interests.

She brought Italian landscapes from her childhood home in San Francisco and hung them strategically throughout the house. Next to them rested Anders' paintings as well as a few of her own creations, and the effect was delightfully eclectic. She collected photography—hanging wedding pictures and family gatherings in groups displayed at eye-level. She bought a handful of area rugs in crimson, green, and gold and laid them under mahogany tables adorned with lamps and porcelain, which complemented the white-marble fireplace at the end of the living room. Leather wing-backed chairs and damask-upholstered settees added comfort throughout, yet the overall effect remained spacious and airy.

With painstaking detail, Valeria composed every room in the house with a flowing color scheme, uniting the upstairs with the downstairs by the sweeping Mediterranean-tile staircase. Once ascended, the stairs ended where a long hallway began. Halfway down the hall, a window encased in wrought-iron looked out to a garden below, right before the guest bedroom door, and at the end of the hall lay the master bedroom. The bedroom carried an elevated view of the sea through the frame of a bay window where oak trees partially obstructed the immediate grounds below. The garden stretched from the back of the house and wrapped itself around to the northern side. When guests came to stay, they remarked upon the fact the sea could be glimpsed from three sides of the house, while the garden remained lush no matter the time of year.

The Kristiansens were surrounded by an impressive array of friends and acquaintances, for Carmel was a new provenance whose people gathered frequently. Friends were easy to come by, and they came in the form of neighbors, town officials, and many of Anders' patrons. As their circle of friends grew, so did Anders' reputation as an artist, and the residents considered the Kristiansens to be people of local importance. They were invited to every party, and Valeria returned the favor by hosting parties of her own which were always the talk of the town. So when the time came to designate who would host Carmel's reception for its first annual Arts Fair, Anders and Valeria were the natural choice.

Upon hearing of their appointment, Valeria rushed off a letter to Francesca, encouraging her to ride the train from San Francisco to the Monterey Peninsula for the big event. She asked her sister to come a few days early to help her with the final details. When she received Francesca's enthusiastic response of compliance, Valeria knew the artists' reception would be a party unlike any other.

"Valeria, we're hosting a reception, not a wedding." Anders reached for her hand. "Are you convinced this is all necessary?" He perused the list Valeria presented him with a skeptical eye. "This is going to cost a king's ransom."

"But only in part for us. The Arts Council will shoulder the majority of the cost. I believe we will set a standard for years to come, so the first artists' reception should be as fine as we can make it."

"Do you think anyone will expect an eight-piece orchestra?" Anders laughed.

"I don't imagine anyone will, but we must have background music to add to the ambience," Valeria enthused. "Just think of it, an orchestra on a slightly raised platform in the back garden, it will be lovely. It will be string music for the most part, the violin, the lute—nothing too overwhelming. We only want something to balance the conversation."

"Far be it from me to become involved in the business of what you know best." Anders handed the list back to Valeria with what looked to be an air of resignation.

"Francesca arrives in three days, so I wanted to have as much organized on my own as I could muster. I feel as if I've thought of everything, but she will spot it if I've left anything out."

"No doubt she will. Between this town and the Sienna sisters, there's a lesson about to be learned regarding the *perfect party*."

* * *

Two hundred and fifty people attended the artists' reception for Carmel's first annual Arts Fair, and as Valeria suspected, Francesca's input proved to be invaluable. Francesca thought of placing a marquee tent across the garden from the orchestra to serve as a receiving area for the artists. Her thought entailed seeing the entire grounds as a whole and distributing the refreshments, musicians, artists, and those who simply wanted to congregate in a way where no element would interfere with another. Consequently, the backyard garden flowed with steady activity, yet there was no danger of congestion.

Everyone dressed gaily, mingling and talking of everything from their families to town gossip—introducing themselves to the artists, drinking champagne, admiring the orchestra, and commenting on the splendid party. The guests stayed until well after midnight, even though Carmel's first official Arts Fair was slated to open early at nine o'clock the following day.

An exhausted Valeria removed her shoes from her aching feet and sat down on the foot of Francesca's bed. A breeze wafted in from the guest bedroom window, and she lifted her hair from her neck to catch the cooling effect.

"I had no way of knowing so many people would attend." Valeria looked at her sister. "Had you not thought of spacing everything the way you did, it might have been an entirely different party."

"Mother always did say to invite so many but prepare for more." Francesca leaned back at the head of the bed. "It seems Carmel has grown since the last time I was here. I only recognized about two dozen people."

"That's very true. Carmel continues to grow by leaps. By any chance, did you happen to meet Mrs. Davenworth's niece?"

"I did meet her. Her name is Ingrid, is it not?"

"Yes, Ingrid Muller. She's lovely. She's married to an American. Ingrid lives in San Luis Obispo and comes up to Carmel regularly with her husband. He has something to do with the railway."

"I figured as much, since she seems to know the region well. Ingrid asked if you and I would be interested in going on a picnic with her the day after tomorrow. We could go down to the beach and make an afternoon of it before I go."

"Oh, Francesca, I hate to think of you leaving. It seems like you always leave too soon."

"Well, I wouldn't want to overstay my welcome, but just the same, I'm pleased to hear you say that. It will make it easier for me to return shortly."

Valeria paused, thinking how much she always missed Francesca and how different their lives had become in the years since her marriage. In most ways, Valeria felt she had come into her own as a woman, as if she now had a purpose in life with a definite role to play, all of which gratified her, but there were times when she longed for the comforts of the past. It took very little for her to summon her feelings of attachment towards Francesca, for in many ways her sister was her anchor. She had spent so many years relying on her for guidance, she didn't think the feeling would ever go away.

"Please tell me you won't stay away too long. Perhaps we could look forward to your return before Christmas."

"I would love that. We should think about encouraging Mother and Father to come. We could all stay at the Pine Inn in town."

"I will feel better about you leaving in a few days if I can look forward to your return." Valeria stifled a yawn. Rising, she went to her sister and hugged her goodnight.

Chapter Twenty

September 22, 2000
Carmel

"Anna?" Kevin whispered. "What are you doing?"

Anna turned and looked behind her, feeling as if she were emerging from an anesthetic daze. For a split second, she was surprised to find herself at the end of a hall. Moments before, she was certain she had been standing inside a large bedroom. It had been her room, she thought, yet now she was here looking at a closed, large wooden door. Her heart raced as she began to walk to the top of the stairs where Kevin was cautiously approaching. A moment later they stood face-to-face, her right hand gripping the rail.

"What are you doing?" Kevin asked again. "Are there guest rooms up here?"

"No, I don't think so. There are only two rooms from what I can tell."

"Then come on, let's go down. We're probably not supposed to be in this part of the hotel." He turned and began to descend the stairs.

She followed him and together they crossed the foyer. She had the uncanny feeling she had swept across this entry many times before, but the feeling grew weaker. She felt the need to hold her breath, although there was nobody around, the front desk in the lobby having been vacated hours before. They walked down the short flight of stairs in the back and out the door that led through the garden to their room.

Once inside, Anna sat down on the bed and looked up at Kevin. "This is going to sound strange," she attempted.

Kevin unloaded his coat pockets of wallet, phone, and keys, placed them on the round table by the door then turned slowly and looked at her.

"What is?"

Anna exhaled. "I think this place is haunted."

"What makes you say that?"

"It's just a feeling I have. I don't know. It feels like I'm being watched or something. Maybe I'm seeing things."

"Watched by whom?"

"That's just it, I don't know."

Kevin returned to the business of taking off his coat and folding it over a chair.

"I swear, when I was in the lobby I felt like I was being pulled to climb the stairs. When I got to the top, I felt like I already knew what was up there."

"So what was up there?" Kevin asked.

"A hallway with a big stained-glass window."

"And two rooms," he added.

"Yes. One of them had a big wooden cathedral-shaped door. It was locked. I tried to open it."

"Anna, you're not supposed to go snooping around in areas that are obviously off-limits to guests." Kevin sounded serious.

"I know, but I was curious. Actually, it went beyond curiosity. I felt like I should, as if I had every right to open that door."

"Why did you feel like you had the right? What does

that mean?"

"I don't know. It just felt familiar to me, as if I'd opened that door a million times before. The thing is, I don't know if I actually opened it or not. I got dizzy for a minute and then I felt as if I were standing in the room, looking out over the yard. Then the whole scene became something else entirely. It felt like I was standing there watching a scene play out, or that somebody was standing there watching me watch a scene."

"What do you mean by somebody?" Kevin frowned. "You were being watched by whom?"

"It felt like I was being watched by *myself.*"

Chapter Twenty-one

September, 22, 1907
Carmel

The door to the master bedroom was thrown wide open, as was the door to the guest room where Francesca stood going through the clothes she'd folded into the chest of drawers. The sisters called back and forth through the hallway while they both dressed, just as they used to do when they were growing up.

"Where is Anders?" Francesca called.

"He went to the coffee shop on Ocean Avenue. All of the men go there in the mornings. I don't know what they do there other than visit and read the paper, but it seems to bond them all," Valeria returned.

"That's because most of them are artists without actual offices. I think artists have to become creative in order to find reason to get up in the morning and leave the house," Francesca pointed out.

"Carmel is not like San Francisco in that way. Precious few are actually businessmen here, the rest are the creative sort, but it makes for such a fascinating cast of characters at parties."

"I believe you. From what I witnessed the other night, I am convinced. You'll find no men like Giancarlo Vargas down here." With that, both girls started laughing, for Giancarlo Vargas had become a standing joke between them.

Francesca walked into Valeria's bedroom. "Do you

know what father tried to do three times since the last time I was down here?"

"What?" Valeria finished arranging the pillows on the master bed.

"Father went out of his way to arrange a chance meeting between Mr. Vargas and me, and he asked him to dinner twice." Francesca sat down on the chaise lounge that graced the area of the bedroom before the bay window.

"Oh, no! Poor you," Valeria put in immediately.

"Now that you are married, I think Father realized if he wants to have an Italian son-in-law, he'd better orchestrate it himself. Sometimes I think he is still baffled at how you and Anders came together."

"Father and everybody else in San Francisco," Valeria said, and both girls laughed until their laughter almost turned into hysterics.

"Can't you just see it? Me besotted with the arrogant Mr. Vargas and him with me? The only thing I know about him is that he is the president of his own fan club. He is so impressed with his position at the Genoa Hotel that he is beside himself."

"And he has Father to thank for it," Valeria added.

"That's right. So the least he could do is marry his single daughter!"

"This is too funny." Valeria continued laughing. "I'm sure you found a way to discourage the pair of them."

"Yes, of course I did. I had to before it went another step further."

"How did you accomplish it?"

"Why, I got Mother involved, of course."

"Smart thinking, Francesca."

"It worked. I wish you could have been there. Mother was like a work of art."

"Tell me what she said."

Francesca put on her best Italian accent. "Now, Domenico, if you want an example of a relationship that will not take root, then just keep doing what you seem to think you have not been detected doing with Giancarlo Vargas and there you will have it."

"I love it," Valeria said. "So typical of Mother."

"Is it not? It put an end to it right then and there. We can both learn something from our mother. She never tells Father what to do. She only makes the slightest suggestion of what he *shouldn't* do."

"It is a formula for success!" Valeria said, still laughing. "We need to get going. Ingrid will be here in under an hour. It'll be really hot today for this time of year so let's wear our bathing attire. We may want to get in the water."

"Then I'll just go back and change my clothes. I will only be a minute, then let's go down and get some coffee while we wait for Ingrid," Francesca suggested.

* * *

The house was quiet in the ten o'clock hour save for the Kristiansens' cook who manned the gas stove, boiling water for coffee. Valeria pulled cups and saucers down from the pantry and placed them on the kitchen table, waiting for Francesca.

"Will you need the picnic basket this morning, Mrs. Kristiansen?"

"I will, thank you, Bridget. It will be the three of us. I'd be grateful if you would make some finger sandwiches, and put some grapes and a thermos of iced tea in there as well. We'll need plates, napkins, salt and pepper, silverware—nothing too heavy because we'll be carrying it down to the beach."

"I'll have that ready for you in a few minutes," Bridget said, her Irish lilt ringing.

Francesca walked into the kitchen carrying a large woolen blanket. "Will this be big enough?"

"Oh, yes, anything will do. Ingrid said she would bring an umbrella, so I think we will be all set. It doesn't matter to me if I sit on the sand or not, in fact, I prefer it. Here is your coffee."

Francesca pulled out one of the kitchen chairs and sat down. "Tell me again how Ingrid fits into Mrs. Davenworth's life. She is her niece, is she not?"

"Yes, Mrs. Davenworth's brother's child. Ingrid is another Norwegian who married an American and ended up in California, just like Mrs. Davenworth. I believe her husband is in some sort of import business that involves the railway. It is interesting how there are similarities within families," Valeria mused.

"That always seems to be the case. I wonder if that means I too will meet and marry a Norwegian."

"Perhaps it will only be another artist. That would be enough."

"Since you have said that, it will no doubt happen," Francesca replied with a laugh.

"Why do you say that?"

"Because you have an uncanny knack for predicting the future, that is why, and you know it as well as I. You are just like Mother in that way. Both of you tend to know things ahead of time."

"Well, since I just said similarities run in families, I

will not dispute you." Valeria poured milk in her coffee and looked at the clock. "I do hope Ingrid arrives on time. I should be back at the house by four-thirty to pay our gardener, Jimmy."

"And meself as well," Bridget chimed in. She was not a cook who discreetly blended in with the background while her employer was in the room, but Valeria was still startled to realize she had been listening.

"Yes, of course, Bridget, I know the weekend is coming. I'll be sure to return from the beach before you leave today."

Bridget nodded. "Thank you, ma'am."

The front doorbell chimed in four octaves, and Valeria quickly left the kitchen and walked across the foyer to admit Ingrid.

"Come in, Ingrid, it is so nice to see you again. Francesca and I are having coffee in the kitchen. May I serve you a cup?"

"Oh, thank you, Valeria, but no. I am saturated with my own morning coffee already." Ingrid placed a large canvas umbrella beside the door and handed Valeria a quilted bag. "I've brought us some chocolates for the picnic. I believe you are partial to chocolate, or so I hear from your husband."

"My husband loves to share my vices with everyone, but today I will not hold it against him and will graciously accept." Valeria smiled. "Thank you, Ingrid. How nice of you. Let's go into the kitchen and gather everything together for the day, shall we?"

Ingrid wielded the large umbrella expertly, for she shared the family characteristics of height and athletic prowess that ran abundantly in the Jorgensen blood-line.

She followed Valeria into the kitchen and greeted Francesca, remarking on how fortuitous it was that both of them should find themselves in Carmel on the same weekend.

"The Arts Council party was splendid, absolutely spectacular, and I understand you had a hand in it," Ingrid said to Francesca.

"I did little more than confirm my sister's ideas. Actually, it was all Valeria's vision."

"What a gift vision is. Since the beginning of time itself, writers, painters, and soothsayers have all benefited from vision. I commend you, Valeria, it was a wonderful party."

The three women walked out the back door and through the garden to the steps that met the road behind the house. It was a short walk, but they each carried something burdensome and had to adjust and readjust many times before their feet found the little path leading to the sand.

As was her habit, Valeria bent down and removed her shoes before she walked upon the sand, so she handed Francesca the picnic basket. "Here, take this for just a little while, I'm tired of carrying it. Let's get down to the water's edge and set everything up there."

"Oh, no, you don't." Francesca deflected the basket. "It's too long a walk on this sand and you're stronger than I am. Anyway, I'm older than you are and much more tired today. Take the basket back."

"Oh, there's nothing like a good sibling quarrel!" Ingrid laughed, and taking the blanket from Francesca's arms, she carried it down to the water's edge and spread it upon the sand. "Francesca, if you are really tired, I'd like to warn you about the sea current today. My husband read a surf report to me before I left this morning and mentioned that there are rip currents, which can be very tricky."

"I've never heard of a rip current."

"They're hard to spot because they're below the surface of the water. There are tides that move in the opposite direction of the shore, and they can literally carry you out to sea," Ingrid explained. "We should all be careful."

"Nothing to concern myself with," Francesca said. "I am not a swimmer, only a wader."

"Well then, Valeria and I can teach you a little today," Ingrid offered. "Let's lie down for a while before we go in the water, shall we?"

They lay side-by-side, stretched out on the soft white sand, and luxuriated in the warmth of the September sun. All around them, men and women walked the shore dressed in their fashionable swimwear. The men wore striped short-sleeved shirts with matching trunks, and the women wore short flouncy sleeveless dresses with hats and coordinating parasols. Some swam and others only tested the water.

It wasn't long before the three women decided to do the same. They walked into the ocean, with both Valeria and Ingrid securing Francesca's hands. They taught her to jump over the swell of incoming waves with a spring strong enough to clear the top of the wave, and they didn't go in further than their waists until Ingrid felt a measure of safety and encouraged Francesca to become a little more daring.

"Allow yourself to float on top of the wave," Ingrid

called to Francesca. "Try to lie on your back for a minute and relax. Just take your feet off the bottom and lean back, the water will support you."

Francesca lay on her back and bobbed on top of the water, reaching out her arms and kicking her feet to keep herself afloat.

"Valeria, look," Francesca raised her voice over the waves, "I'm doing it! I'm actually swimming!"

Valeria waved a hand at her sister. "Yes, I can see that, good for you, Francesca!" she called back. "I'm going in now. Come in out of the water when you get ready and we'll have our picnic."

Valeria and Francesca found Ingrid to be a wonderful companion and the conversation flowed effortlessly as they lingered over their picnic. Ingrid talked about her childhood in Norway, regaling them with stories of the Jorgensen family, which was a subject that fascinated Valeria. Afterwards, they walked along the beach covering the entire length of Carmel Bay. They stopped and talked to passing strangers who walked their dogs off-leash. After placing wagers on who could reach the heights first, they climbed the white sand dunes to their very tops before running back down.

When they returned to their blanket, they lay down and watched the clouds stream across the sky as the afternoon began to deepen. Once or twice, Valeria noticed a lull in the conversation and looked over to find Francesca dozing in the lowering sun.

"Valeria," Ingrid whispered, "don't you have to go back to the house?"

"Yes, I suppose I should get going. I can just run up there and come right back. I won't be long, only about twenty minutes or so. You can stay here with Francesca. I haven't the heart to disturb her. We can watch the sunset when I return."

Valeria picked her shoes up from the sand and retraced her steps across the beach homeward. She laced them at the path that met the road, turned left and walked to the steps that led into the garden. The back door to the kitchen was open and when she walked in, she saw Anders talking to Bridget.

"How was the beach?" Anders placed a light kiss on Valeria's cheek.

"Ingrid and Francesca are still down there. I just came back to the house to see Bridget and Jimmy off, then I'll return and we're all going to watch the sunset. Would you like to join us?"

"Thank you for the invitation to your female club, but no, thank you. I'm going into the garden to have a talk with Jimmy. I'll see to him for you and will be here when you return." Anders kissed her again and left for the front lawn.

* * *

Down at the beach, the sun descended towards the ocean in hovering increments above the distant waterline. Ingrid turned lazily, trying to gauge its eventual demise. She figured there would only be another half-hour of sunlight at the very most, so she decided to wake the sleeping Francesca.

Soon Valeria would return, and if Francesca would help her put everything back in the basket and fold the beach blanket, then the two of them could spend the remaining moments of sunlight with Valeria, just as they had planned. They could witness the sun disappearing in the distance and have ample time to return to the house before darkness prevailed.

"Francesca?" Ingrid reached out a hand and touched her on her shoulder. "Wake up."

Francesca turned and smiled at Ingrid. "Did I fall asleep? I didn't mean to. Where's Valeria? Did she go back to the house?"

"She did. She'll be back in a minute. Let's gather everything together before she returns."

Francesca stood up and stretched her back. "I feel like walking into the water for just a minute. Will you join me? I need to wake up."

"Oh no, you go ahead. I don't think I am as warm-blooded as you and your sister seem to be. The water gives me a chill I'd rather not carry for the rest of the evening."

Francesca walked to the water's edge and stood looking out at the horizon. It seemed unlimited in its expanse, and the blue-gray water stretched between the shore and the sky like liquid silver with hues of dark green and blue that looked so enticing she wanted to immerse herself in the middle of the swirling colors.

She turned around to wave at Ingrid and saw her forty yards or so away with her back turned, talking to a woman who held a child's hand. She turned back to the water and walked in up to her ankles.

At first, the water was startlingly cold but she quickly grew used to the temperature and decided it was refreshingly pleasant. She waded in up to her knees and stood still, feeling the sand beneath her feet erode dramatically, yet she stayed firm as the rushing water beat out a rhythm that pulsated to and fro, to and fro. She walked a few paces forward, and the sand beneath her feet became firm again, so she allowed the water to rise up to her waist while she bounced up and down, enjoying the brief moments when she felt her whole body suspended by water, entirely free of gravity. The feeling reminded her of the time she and Valeria went over to their neighbor's house when they were very young, where they had jumped on a trampoline for the very first time.

Up and down Francesca sprang, buoyant in the salty waves, pointing her toes each time they left the sand. She took little notice that she had made forward progress, but when water reached the top of her chest, she realized her feet were no longer finding the sand. She bore her full weight downwards, searching for ground to stand on, and thought she found it once, but there was an eddy scattering the moving sand beneath her feet, so she stretched out her arms and tried with everything she had to keep her weight aloft.

She wanted to turn towards the beach and began to panic when she realized she couldn't turn, for the rhythm of the water was incessant and had grown from a gentle pulse to a jolting movement she couldn't keep time with in any manner that would help. She was being thrown back, yet she couldn't stop her arms from their automatic response of trying to propel her forward in their attempt at conquering the crashing momentum.

Twice her head went under, but she reached her arms overhead and willed them to pull her up through the combative water. Every ounce of strength she had went towards keeping her head above water, for the struggle to breathe was her only priority. Her head was repeatedly thrust back, and although she caught glimpses of the sky, waves stronger than her efforts slammed over her then contracted into themselves, thrashing her forward and down, pulling her forward and down repeatedly. She had the gasping reserve to resist until a burning sensation filled her chest, and she knew instantly she had swallowed water.

Her arms atrophied, and she was completely overpowered when, horrifically, another wave wracked her body and pinned her backwards. With one last glimpse of the sky, Francesca succumbed, melded into the water, and helplessly let go.

* * *

Valeria thanked Bridget for her week's work, paid her appropriately, and walked slowly up the stairs towards the upstairs hall. It was growing cooler outside, and she decided to bring a wrap down to the beach with her. As she climbed the stairs, her legs felt the effects from all the romping at the beach, and she wondered if Ingrid and Francesca were feeling the same.

She smiled, thinking of her sister trying to learn how to swim, and couldn't wait to write her parents telling them of the day's events. She knew they would be surprised, for she herself was the better athlete of the sisters, and of the two times their father had tried to teach Francesca to swim, Francesca had shown very little interest.

Valeria opened the guest bedroom door to let a little air in, then crossed to the draperies and pulled them apart, letting in the last of the daylight. When she was satisfied the room was tidy, she walked back through the hall and entered her bedroom. She pulled open the armoire and located a cashmere shawl warm enough to keep the chill of the setting sun off her skin. Arranging it around her shoulders, she turned towards the door then stopped abruptly, listening.

It came like the wail of a banshee from somewhere out in the yard. Valeria rushed over to the bay window, rounded the chaise lounge, and frantically tried to locate the mounting noise. For a split second, she thought it was the howl of an animal, but it grew louder and closer. She scanned the yard below the window in three directions until she saw what appeared to be movement through the oak branches that partially obstructed her view. A few seconds of anxiety and confusion lapsed, then into her vision ran a screaming, hysterical Ingrid, full speed and holding her skirts above her knees, the better to race towards the house.

"Anders!" Valeria shrieked. "Anders! Something is wrong!" She flew through the hall and ran down the length of the stairs.

"Anders, where are you?" Valeria raced through the foyer, her heart throbbing in her chest, her voice taking on a pitch and quality she didn't identify as her own. She threw open the kitchen door and saw Anders stabilizing a frantically disoriented Ingrid by her shoulders.

"You left her?" Anders demanded. "Are you certain she has drowned?"

"I had to come get you," Ingrid wailed. "Oh, come quickly. Anders, I am so sorry, I did not know what else to do. You must come now. Francesca is lying on the sand. There are a few people with her who saw her in the water before I did. They helped me pull her out. I only turned my back for a minute. Anders, I had to leave her. I had to immediately come to you."

"Jimmy!" Anders bellowed, and within seconds Jimmy was urgently dispatched into town to summon the doctor.

Anders, Ingrid, and Valeria rushed immediately to the beach. Francesca lay prone, her dark wet hair in tangles across her face, her eyes half-open. There was no life-force in her body—it was apparent from the second Valeria dropped to her knees beside her. She smoothed the hair from Francesca's face and doubled over, laying her sobbing head on her sister's chest.

She was distraught, she was horrified, she was catatonic, she felt guilty, she felt responsible. She should never have gone back to the house when she did. She should never have left Francesca's side. She should have awakened Francesca and had her come with her. They always did everything together. Why oh why had she made an exception this time? She couldn't believe this had happened.

"Please, God! I didn't mean it, I didn't mean to leave her side. Can't I do this once again? I made a mistake, I wasn't thinking. Please, God, don't make me pay the price." It was too terrible to comprehend. "Francesca, wake up!" Valeria implored again and again.

Valeria turned to Ingrid. "Where?" she screamed. "I want you to point out to me exactly where she was, where did this happen? Why were you not with her? You know she can't swim!"

"My back was not turned long," Ingrid defended. "She said she was only going in to wade for a minute. It happened so quickly. She was just right there," she pointed, "right there in front of that large rock. Valeria, I am so sorry."

Valeria turned and marked the rock in her memory at the exact time the doctor confirmed the fatal news. No amount of resuscitation would revive Francesca, and Valeria stood transfixed, staring out into the ocean at the place where Francesca drowned.

It is trapped now. The death of my dear sister is trapped in this place and it will now be a portal in time.

Chapter Twenty-two

September 22, 2000
Carmel

Because she was still rattled from the strange vision she'd had at the top of the stairs, Anna was afraid to sleep that night. She was afraid to close her eyes and enter the dream-state because she considered it to be another dimension. She was afraid of the thought of other dimensions because she knew she was sensitive and therefore susceptible to their influences. Always there was the nagging question within her of what would happen if she walked through the door of the dream-state and couldn't return.

She thought about alternate realities and considered the possibility that no one could really say which one was more real than the other. Maybe waking reality was the dream, and dreams were in fact reality. She didn't want to spend too much time on the conundrum because she knew in the moment she was in bed at the Madeira Hotel in Carmel, and Kevin lay beside her. That was where she wanted to keep her focus. That was what was important to her now.

She lay in bed and watched the shadows on the wall change shape as the wind rustled the bougainvillea on the patio outside the window. She let her eyes scan the darkened room, covering every inch of it from the ceiling to the outline of the room's furniture. She heard Kevin breathing beside her, lost in his own dream world. She started to wonder what he was dreaming.

She looked at the digital clock by her bedside; it was nearly midnight. She went through her prayers of gratitude and petition, and played pictures before her mind's eye of the life she wanted to create, for she was a great believer in creative visualization as well as the power of positive thought. She turned over on her right side, gathered the blankets closer around her, and fell lightly into sleep…

* * *

She walked down a lane, braced against the gusting wind that twisted her skirts into tangles around her ankles. She saw herself sweeping her long dark hair to the left and clasping it firmly in the same hand that held the top of her cloak. Determinedly, she marched forward until the lane veered to a sharp right and headed straight down to the sea. When she reached the place where the lane met the sand, she leaned over quickly and removed her lace-up shoes. Securing them tightly in her right hand, she walked onto the beach, barely breaking its surface.

The waves came forward in a mounting swell and with their forward progression, more of the beach disappeared into the steel-gray of the Pacific Ocean. It was the end of the day, and the tide labored forcibly beneath the fading blue sky. She stood listening intently to the fury of the wind as it intermittently drowned out the pulsating rhythm of the sea.

Gathering herself, she turned to the right, to the place in the water she had come to see. Shielding her eyes from the setting sun, she steadied her gaze and spoke into the wind as a chill began to creep up her spine.

"This place will now be a portal in time," she said.

* * *

Anna sprang bolt-upright in bed and screamed into the darkness from the depth of her soul's memory.

"Francesca, wake up!"

Author Acknowledgements

Many thanks to Joseph Francis Fullerton, who encouraged me to write this book.

And unending thanks to Jennie Muller, an unforgettable woman, for her unwavering friendship and support.

To Kelly Fisher in Nashville for her friendship and enthusiasm, and to Maria Newman; thanks to both for reading the first draft of this book.

To Tama Dudley Harris and Louise Ruth Pidgeon because they are part of "one of us."

To Neville L. Johnson and Ilyssa Adler in Los Angeles for their stellar counsel.

And always, to Shirley, Tom, TJF and Haines.

About the Author

Claire Fullerton is a two-time, award-winning essayist, a newspaper columnist and a contributing editor for numerous magazines. She hails from Memphis, Tennessee and now divides her time between Malibu and Carmel-By-The-Sea, California with her husband, two German shepherds, and two black cats.

Claire is a Ballet dancer, a Pilates teacher, and a former radio disc-jockey who is feverishly at work on her second novel.

Readers can learn more about Claire and her upcoming books by visiting her website at www.clairefullerton.com.

If you enjoyed A Portal in Time, you might enjoy another time travel romance, Bridge to the Past by Judith Ingram.

Victoria longs for a different life. Then her wish on a mysterious coin transports her back in time, into the body of a ruthless young woman accused of murdering her husband... Despite the perils of her new identity, Victoria discovers a new sense of belonging and adventure in the other woman's world, especially when a handsome man captures her attention. But can borrowed love last for a lifetime? And how long will Victoria's wish last?

Available now! For more details, visit our website at http://vinspirepublishing.com/book_pages/bridgetothepast.html

Plan Your Next Escape!
What's Your Reading Pleasure?

Whether it's brawny Highlanders, intriguing mysteries, young adult romance, illustrated children's books, or uplifting love stories, Vinspire Publishing has the adventure for you!

For a complete listing of books available, visit our website at www.vinspirepublishing.com.

Like us on Facebook at
www.facebook.com/VinspirePublishing

Follow us on Twitter at
www.twitter.com/vinspire2004

and join our newsletter for details of our upcoming releases, giveaways, and more!
http://t.co/46UoTbVaWr

We are your travel guide to your next adventure!

CPSIA information can be obtained at www.ICGtesting.com
Printed in the USA
BVOW03s1855210414

351273BV00002B/8/P

9 780989 063227